單字急救包

急救包

First-Aid
Vocabulary

國家圖書館出版品預行編目資料

單字急救包 / 陳久娟編著
-- 二版. -- 新北市：雅典文化，民106. 06
面 ； 公分. -- (行動學習；11)
ISBN 978-986-5753-83-2(平裝附光碟片)
1. 英語　2. 詞彙
805. 12　　　　　　　　　　　　　　106005311

行動學習系列 11

單字急救包

編著／陳久娟
內文排版／王國卿
封面設計／姚恩涵

法律顧問：方圓法律事務所／涂成樞律師

總經銷：永續圖書有限公司　　CVS代理／美璟文化有限公司
永續圖書線上購物網　　　　　TEL：(02) 2723-9968
www.foreverbooks.com.tw　　 FAX：(02) 2723-9668

出版日／2017年06月

雅典文化

出版社
22103　新北市汐止區大同路三段194號9樓之1
TEL　(02) 8647-3663
FAX　(02) 8647-3660

● 序言

　　這是一本袖珍單字手冊，內容包羅萬象，您可以塞在袋裡，放在車上，或是擱在角落。不管是等公車的通勤族，培養情緒好蹲馬桶，還是任何時候想充實一下，隨手從包包裡，角落中抽出本書，就可以利用瑣碎的時間進修。

　　單字急救包有最完整的單字內容，最人性化的印刷排版，最便利的包裝方式。同時，它也是一本工具書，提供您最簡便的查詢介面，從頁面側邊即可很快找出您需要的單字。

　　有了本書，您不需要騰出大把時間枯坐書桌前背單字，英文便可以在無形中進步喔！

• Chapter 1 吃的語言

● Chapter 2 玩樂休閒

服飾統稱

鞋類及服裝

香水飾品

頭髮

● Chapter 3 生活常識I

命理占星

生活用語

生活空間

文具用品

● Chapter 4 生活常識 Ⅱ

常用符號

數學運算

數字詞彙

幾何詞彙

常用單位及度量衡

各國宗教

節日習俗

大眾運輸工具

交通號誌標語

● Chapter 5 生理衛生

情緒表達

形容個性常用詞

身體動作

成長發育

• Chapter 6 商用英語

商用英語

業務英語

價格談判

辦公室英語

辦公室設備

書信及電話

會議英語

評論數據

● Chapter 7 國際金融

銀行財會

• Chapter 8 新鮮人專區

口語報告

校園稱謂

學校制度

科系課程

Chapter

1

吃的語言

● 吃的語言

口感

chewy	有嚼勁的	001
crispy	酥脆的	
crunchy	鬆脆的	
rich	口味濃郁的	
creamy	似乳質的 濃郁膏狀的	
mushy	糊狀的	
tough	硬的(形容肉質)	
juicy	多汁的	
soft	鬆軟	
smooth	滑順	
strong	很濃(形容味道)	
greasy oily	油膩	
fresh	新鮮	
garlicky	大蒜味	
light	清淡	
tender	柔軟，嫩的	

形容好吃

yummy tasty delicious	美味極了
nice good	味道不錯
delicious	美味的

形容不好吃

bad tasting	難吃	(002)
disgusting	好噁心	
yuck		
gross		
nasty		
awful		
interesting	味道好奇怪	
funny		
weird		
strange		
tasteless	沒什麼味道	
unsavory		
weak		
disgusting	噁心	
stinky	臭	

食物的調味

sweet	甜
salty	鹹
sour	酸
acid	
tart	
spicy	辣
too spicy	太辣了，辣死了
bitter	苦
dry	苦(形容酒類)

食物的成分

vitamin	維生素
vitamin A	維生素 A
vitamin B12	維生素 B12
vitamin B6	維生素 B6
vitamin C	維生素 C
vitamin D	維生素 D
vitamin E	維生素 E
folic acid	葉酸
mineral	礦物質
phosphorus	磷
potassium	鉀
sodium	鈉
sulphur	硫磺
manganese	錳
magnesium	鎂
iodine	碘
iron	鐵
chlorine	氯
cobalt	鈷
copper	銅
calcium	鈣
fluorine	氟
fat	脂肪
calorie	卡路里
carbohydrate	碳水化合物，醣
starch	澱粉

sucrose	蔗糖	(003)
fatty acid	脂肪酸	
fructose	果糖	
galactose	半乳糖	
glucose	葡萄糖	
nutrition	營養	
protein	蛋白質	
carotene	胡蘿蔔素	
roughage	纖維素	
cellulose	植物纖維素	
dietary fiber	食物纖維	
lactic acid	乳酸	
lactose	乳糖	
lipid	脂質	
lipoprotein	脂蛋白	
triglyceride	三酸甘油脂	
cholesterol	膽固醇	
low-calorie	低卡	
low-carb	低碳水化合物	
low-fat	低脂	
fat-soluble vitamin	脂溶性維生素	
water-soluble vitamin	水溶性維生素	

● 外食

上餐館

snack bar	速食店
catering	承辦酒席 提供飲食服務
food court	購物中心裡的美食街或泛指有攤位及桌子，供人飲食的區域。
self-serve dining	自助餐飲
buffet	快餐，小吃店
diner	火車上的餐車 路邊的小販
food stand	攤販
night market	夜市
restaurant	餐廳
make a reservation	預訂
full all booked	客滿
Party of 5!	總共有 5 個人！
Table for 5!	五個人的座位！
table is ready	桌子已經準備好了
smoking zone	吸煙區
non smoking zone	非吸煙區
menu manual	菜單
order	點菜

buffet style	自助式	(004)
a la carte	照菜單點菜	
specialty	招牌菜	
today's special	今日特餐	
chef's special	主廚特餐	
vegetarian	素食者	
on diet meal plan	減肥，營養餐	
drink beverage	飲料	
refill	續杯	
doggy bag	把吃剩的食物 打包帶走	
to go	外帶	
for here	內用	
bill	帳單	
Check, Please!	買單！	
separate checks	分開算	
just one check	一起算	
this is on me	算我的	
my treat	我請客	
go Dutch	各自付錢	
cash	現金	
credit card	信用卡	
tip	小費	
receipt	收據	

蛋的煮法

sunny-side up	單煎一面的荷包蛋
scrambled egg	炒蛋
fried egg	荷包蛋
easy over	兩面煎 (蛋黃半熟)
over hard	全熟蛋 兩面煎 (蛋黃全熟)
soft-boiled egg	半熟的水煮蛋
hard-boiled egg	煮得全熟的蛋
poached egg	蒸蛋
omelet	煎蛋捲
omelette	蛋捲

牛排的煮法

well done	全熟
medium well	稍為熟一點的
medium	適中偏生的
medium rare	三分熟的
rare	較生的

甜點

pudding	布丁
ice cream	霜淇淋
chocolate	巧克力口味
strawberry	草莓口味
vanilla	香草口味

ice sucker	冰棒	(005)
pie	餡餅	
apple pie	蘋果派	
tart	水果餡餅，水果塔	
pastry	點心	
cake	蛋糕	
cream cake	奶油蛋糕	
shortcake	水果酥餅	
jello, jelly	果凍	
yam	甜薯	
sweet potato	番薯	
raisin	葡萄乾	
cookie	餅乾	
biscuit	(英)餅乾 (美)小麵包	
candy(美)	糖果	
sweets(英)	糖果	
candy cane	拐杖糖	

fortune cookie

幸運餅乾，打開後有張小紙條，上面寫著各種勉勵的話。在國外中國餐館常見。

軟性飲料

grande	大杯
tall	中杯
short	小杯
beverage	飲料

soft drink	非酒精 軟性飲料
mineral water	礦泉水
Latte	拿鐵
Espresso	義式濃縮
Cappuccino	卡布奇諾
Café Mocha	摩卡咖啡
Café Au Lait	咖啡歐蕾
decaf	低咖啡因
low fat	低脂
non fat	無脂
decaf	低咖啡因
black coffee	黑咖啡 (不加糖的咖啡)
plain coffee	純咖啡
instant coffee	即溶咖啡
white coffee	牛奶咖啡
coffee with cream and sugar	加奶精及糖的咖啡
decaffeinated coffee	低咖啡因的咖啡
hot chocolate	熱巧克力
tea	茶
green tea	綠茶
black tea	紅茶
jasmine tea	茉莉花茶

earl grey tea	伯爵茶	(006)
mint tea	薄荷茶	
lavender tea	薰衣草茶	
camomile tea	菊花茶	
Assam black tea	阿薩姆紅茶	
milk tea	奶茶	
English breakfast tea		
	英式早餐茶	
milk	牛奶	
tea bag	茶袋，茶包	
fruit juice	果汁	
lemonade	檸檬汁	
orangeade	橘子汁	
orange juice	柳橙汁	
fruit punch	混合水果飲料	
non-alcoholic cocktail		
	無酒精雞尾酒	
cider	蘋果西打	

酒精飲料

beer	啤酒
light beer	淡啤酒
draft beer	生啤酒
stout beer	黑啤酒
champagne	香檳酒
punch	潘趣酒
wine	葡萄酒

liquor	烈酒
aperitif	葡萄酒，開胃酒
white wine	白葡萄酒
red wine	紅葡萄酒，紅酒
Sherry	雪利酒
Martini	馬丁尼
Vermouth	苦艾酒
Whisky	威士忌
Brandy	白蘭地
Scotch	蘇格蘭威士忌
Vodka	伏特加
Gin	琴酒
Tequila	龍舌蘭酒

氣泡式飲料

carbonated beverage	碳酸飲料
Pepsi Cola	百事可樂
Diet Pepsi	無糖百事可樂
Diet	健怡可樂
cocacola, coke	可口可樂
7-up	七喜
sprite	雪碧
soda water sparkling water	蘇打水
Tonic	無糖氣泡水
coke light	低熱量可樂
Perrier	沛綠雅氣泡 礦泉水

| sparkling water | 氣泡礦泉水 | (007) |
| apple cider | 蘋果西打 | |

● 自理餐點

烹調的方式

cookery	烹調法
boil	水煮
fry	煎
stir fry	炸
deep fry	炒
scalded	燙煮的
stewed	燉的
simmer	文火燉
	煨
braised with soy sauce	
	紅燒的
braise	燜
steam	蒸
smoked	燻的
toasted	烤(麵包)
baked	烘的(麵包)
grilled	鐵盤烤的
roasted	烤的(肉類)
broiled	燒烤的
drain	撈乾
	曬乾

dried	乾的
iced	冰鎮的

食材的處理

shell	剝 剝皮
peel	削皮
slice	切片
shred	切絲
mashed	搗爛的
ground	磨碎的
beat	打
toss	擲
knead	捏(麵糰) 和(麵糰)
minced	絞成末的
chopped	切碎的
diced	切小方塊
carved	切好的
frozen	冰凍的

煮熟的程度

cooked	煮熟的
all cooked	全熟的
all done	全熟的
well done	熟透的
underdone	半生不熟的

burnt	燒焦了的	(008)
raw	生的 未煮的	

食物的新鮮度

fresh	新鮮的
ruined	食物壞掉了
ripe	(水果)熟了
stale	陳腐的 變壞了的
spoiled	壞掉的
rotten	腐壞的
spoiled odor	腐敗的氣味
spoiled odor	
moldy	發霉的

調味料

seasoning	調味品
salt	鹽
sugar	糖
brown sugar	紅糖
dark brown sugar	黑糖
rock sugar	冰糖
cubic suger	方糖
icing sugar	糖粉 糖霜
pepper	胡椒粉
spice	香料

ketchup	蕃茄醬
cornstarch **corn flower**	太白粉,玉米粉
salad oil	沙拉油
soy sauce	醬油
chilly	辣椒
mustard	芥末
vinegar	醋
barbecue sauce	沙茶醬
cinnamon	肉桂
star anise	八角
cheese	起司
jam	果醬
butter	奶油
caviar	魚子醬
cube sugar	方糖
ginger	薑
green onion	蔥
spring onion	蔥
garlic	大蒜
basil	羅勒
coriander	香菜
chili	辣椒
sesame oil	麻油
oyster sauce	蠔油
olive oil	橄欖油
sesame seed	芝麻

red chili powder	辣椒粉	
pepper	胡椒	
sesame paste	芝麻醬	

● 食材種類

蔬果類

dried black mushroom	
	冬菇
pickle	酸菜，泡菜
mushroom	蘑菇
onion	洋蔥
potato	馬鈴薯
carrot	紅蘿蔔
radish	白蘿蔔
spinach	菠菜
cabbage	高麗菜
cucumber	大黃瓜
broccoli	綠色花椰菜
cauliflower	白花菜
red pepper	紅椒
green pepper	青椒
yellow pepper	黃椒
eggplant	茄子
celery	芹菜
white cabbage	包心菜
red cabbage	紫色包心菜

Chinese cabbage	大白菜
watercress	西洋菜
lettuce	萵苣
baby corn	玉米尖
sweet corn	玉米
corn	玉米粒
leek	大蔥
turnip	蕪菁
okra lady's fingers	秋葵
tofu	豆腐
bean curd sheet	腐皮
green bean	綠豆
red bean	紅豆
black bean	黑豆
red kidney bean	大紅豆
peas	碗豆
dwarf bean	四季豆
flat bean	長形平豆
eddoes	小芋頭
taro	大芋頭
sweet potato	蕃薯
tiger lily buds	金針
mu-er	木耳
tomato	蕃茄
lemon	檸檬
peach	桃子

		(010)
orange	橙	
star fruit	楊桃	
cherry	櫻桃	
golden apple	黃綠蘋果	
apple	蘋果	
pear	梨子	
banana	香蕉	
grape	葡萄	
honeydew melon	蜜瓜	
lichee	荔枝	
kiwi	奇異果	
pineapple	鳳梨	
custard apple	釋迦	
grape fruit	葡萄柚	
coconut	椰子	
fig	無花果	
strawberry	草莓	
mango	芒果	

肉類	
pork	豬肉
lard	豬油
pork pieces	瘦豬肉塊
pork steak	無骨豬排
pork chops	連骨豬排
casserole pork	帶骨腿肉
minced steak	絞肉

chop	肉塊
pork fillet	小里肌肉
pork rib	肋骨
spare rib of pork	小排骨
spare rib pork chops	帶骨的瘦肉
pig feet	豬腳
hock	蹄膀
pig liver	豬肝
pig kidney	豬腰 腰子
pig heart	豬心
pig bag	豬肚
pork sausage meat	做香腸的絞肉
smoked bacon	醃肉
bacon	培根
sausage	香腸
beef	牛肉
mimced beef	牛絞肉
shoulder chops	肩肉
chuck steak	頭肩肉 筋油較多
leg beef	牛腱肉
ox tail	牛尾
ox heart	牛心
ox tongue	牛舌
roll	牛腸
cow heel	牛筋

honeycomb tripe	蜂窩牛肚	(011)
tripe	牛肚	
egg	蛋	
chicken	雞肉	
fresh grade leg	大雞腿	
fresh grade breast	雞胸肉	
chicken drumstick	小雞腿	
chicken wing	雞翅膀	
duck	鴨肉	
goose	鵝肉	

海鮮	
lobster	龍蝦
shrimp	蝦
prawn	蝦
peeled prawn	蝦仁
king prawn	大蝦
shrimp	小蝦米
dried shrimp	蝦米
crab	螃蟹
crab stick	蟹肉條
oyster	牡蠣
mussel	淡菜
winkle	田螺
whelk top	小螺肉
cockle	小貝肉

scallop	干貝 扇貝
cod	鱈魚
haddock	鱈魚
hake	鱈魚類
tuna	鮪魚
trout	鱒魚
carp	鯉魚
plaice	比目魚
herring	鯡
mackerel	鯖
salmon	鮭
eel	鰻
octopus	章魚
dressed squid	花枝
squid	烏賊
cod fillet	鱈魚塊
smoked salmon	燻鮭魚
herring roes	鯡魚子
boiled cod roes	鱈魚子
dried fish	魚乾
sea vegetable **sea weed**	海帶

常見食材

meat	肉類
vegetable	蔬菜

sea food	海鮮	(012)
flour	麵粉	

主食類

rice	米飯
noodles	麵條
instant noodles	速食麵
silk noodles	粉絲
rice noodles	米粉
steamed bun	饅頭
steamed bun with stuffing	
	包子
all-purpose flour	中筋麵粉
plain flour	
cake flour	低筋麵粉
soft flour	
weak flour	
low protein flour	
self-raising flour	
gluten flour	高筋麵粉
strong flour	
bread flour	
baker's flour	
high protein flour	
whole wheat flour	全麥麵粉

First-Aid Vocabulary

玩樂休閒

● 服飾統稱

服飾統稱

bag	袋狀物品 (男女通用) (013)
suitcase	手提箱，公事包
wallet	皮夾
purse	女用手提包
shoulder bag	有肩帶的皮包
briefcase	公事包
backpack	登山包，背包
suitcase	小提箱
trunk	大衣箱
shoes	皮鞋
sneakers	運動鞋
top	上衣
skirt	裙子
pants	褲子
suit	西裝，套裝
shirt	襯衫

名牌採購

boutique	精品店
monogram	品牌名稱組成的圖案，例如：**LV** 圖案的經典款提包稱之。
dust bag	防塵袋
designer	設計師，設計名家

● 鞋類及服裝

服裝單字

double-breasted jacket	
	雙排扣西裝外套
single breasted	單排扣
tie	領帶
tie-pin	領帶夾
tuxedo	燕尾服
trousers	西褲(英)
short pants	西短褲
overalls	背帶褲 工作褲
slacks	寬鬆的長褲
socks	襪子
trench coat	風衣
cape	披風
overcoat	大衣
working wear	工作服
evening dress	晚禮服
blouse	女襯衫
dress	女洋裝
vest	背心
slim skirt	窄裙
pantyhose	褲襪

女鞋

dress shoes	精緻鞋，時裝鞋
high-heeled shoes	高跟鞋
Mary Janes	有扣帶的低跟女鞋
boots	靴子
bootee	輕巧女靴
fashion boots	時尚靴
thigh boots	高至大腿的長統靴
knee boots	長統靴
half boots	中統靴
high/mid/low cut	高統/中統/低統靴
chukka boots	高至足踝的靴子
ankle boots	短靴

運動鞋

sport footwear	運動鞋統稱
athletic shoes	運動鞋
casual shoes	便鞋
jogging shoes	慢跑鞋
basketball shoes	籃球鞋
hiking boots	健行靴
travel shoes	旅遊鞋
flaty shoes	平底便鞋
sneakers	膠底帆布運動鞋

特殊用途鞋款

crampon	釘鞋	(015)
sabot	木鞋	
work footwear	工作鞋	
custom shoes	定製鞋	
embroidery shoes	繡花鞋	
roller skate shoes	溜冰鞋	
skiing shoes	滑雪鞋	
skating shoes	滑冰鞋	
jockey boots	騎馬用鞋	
ballet shoes	芭蕾舞鞋	
fishing wader	釣魚鞋	
orthopaedic shoes	矯正鞋	

鞋子的相關零件

sole	鞋底
heels	鞋跟
foot pad	鞋墊
lace	鞋帶
tip	前套

鞋尖

toe	鞋頭
toe cap	鞋頭
tongue	鞋舌
Velcro	魔術帶，黏扣帶
shoe horn	鞋拔

鞋款的設計

shoe designer	鞋子的設計師
shoemaker	鞋匠
latest design	最新的款式
footwear	鞋類
point toe	尖形鞋頭
oval toe	橢圓形鞋頭
round toe	圓形鞋頭
square toe	方形鞋頭
peep toe shoes	露趾尖式
high heels	高跟鞋
too hard	太硬
too soft	太軟
trimmings	飾物
children shoes	童鞋
men's shoes	男鞋
ladies' shoes	淑女鞋
leather shoes	皮鞋

● 香水飾品

香水相關字

wear	擦(香水)
apply	用(香水)
fragrance	香水
cologne	古龍水
aftershave	鬍後水

scent	氣味	(016)
subtle	輕微的 不知不覺的	
strong	強烈的	

香水的種類(由濃至淡)

perfume	濃香水 香料
essence de perfume	香精性香水
eau de parfum	香水 香氛 (濃度較香精低)
eau de toilette	淡香水 (濃度較香水低)
eau de cologne	古龍水，男性香水 (濃度較淡香水低)
eau de fraicheur	清香水 多為體香劑或鬍後水 (濃度最低)

配件

hairpin	釵
headgear	頭飾
earring earbob	耳飾
dangle	有墜子的飾品
dangler	耳飾 晃來晃去的東西
tongue ring	舌環

tongue bar	裝在舌頭上的棒狀飾品
ring	戒指
necklace	項鏈
pendant	項鏈的墜子
brooch	胸針
bracelet	手鏈
brace lace	
navel jewelry	肚臍飾品
belly ring	環狀肚臍飾品
bangle	手鐲
	腳鐲
toe ring	腳趾用戒指

金銀

karat	K 金
platinum	鉑
	白金
plating	鍍金
gold plated	
genuine gold	真金
	赤金
gold bar	金條
gold filled	包金
ornamental gold	飾金
covered silver	鍍銀的
pure silver	純銀的
silver ornament	銀飾

sterling silver	標準純銀 純銀

鑽石水晶

diamond	鑽石
genuine diamond	真鑽
CZ diamond	水鑽
crystal rock crystal	水晶
crystal glass	水晶玻璃
rubasse	紅水晶
amethyst	紫水晶
acicular crystal	髮晶

寶石

gem	寶石 寶物
gemstone	寶石
ruby	紅寶石
garnet	石榴石 夜明珠 深色紅寶石
sapphire	藍寶石
topaz	黃寶石 黃玉 托帕石
synthetic cut stone	人造寶石
amber	琥珀

jade	玉
jadeite	硬玉
	翡翠
emerald	翡翠
	祖母綠
jasper	碧玉
alexandrite	紫翠玉
ivory	象牙
olivine	橄欖石
opal	貓眼石
	蛋白石
cloisonné	景泰藍的

其他珠寶

jewelry shop	珠寶店
enamel	琺瑯
agate	瑪瑙
coral	珊瑚
pearl	珍珠
rosee	桃色珍珠
colored pearl	有色珍珠
natural pearl	天然珍珠
fresh water pearl	淡水珍珠
genuine pearl	珍珠
olivet	人造珍珠
orient	上等珍珠
shell	貝殼

● 頭髮

保養

shampoo	洗髮精	(018)
hair conditioner	潤髮乳	
hair dressing gel	護髮乳	
treatment		
hair pack		
hot oil	熱油保養	
dry	乾燥	
	乾枯髮質	
split	分岔	
split ends		
damage	受損髮質	
brittleness	易斷裂	
breakage	受損	

造型方式

perm	燙髮
perm hair	
dye hair	染髮
trim	修剪
thin	打薄
layer	打層次
cut	剪髮
part	分邊
hairline	髮際線

造型工具

styling gel	造型髮膠
mousse	慕絲
roll	髮捲
roller perm roller crimper	捲髮器
clippers	電推剪
perm formula cold waving lotion	冷燙劑
hairdryer	吹風機
hairgrip	小髮夾
clip	夾子
clamp	鯊魚夾
hairpin	髮簪
snood	網狀帽
hairnet	髮網

鬍子造型

beard	山羊鬍
full beard	大鬍子
mustache	小鬍子
whisker	落腮鬍
goatee	山羊鬍子
tile beard	瓦形鬍
military moustache	軍人鬍
stubble beard	殘鬚 鬍渣

各種髮型

hairdo	女子髮型	
hairstyle		
crop	平頭	
crew cut		
flattop		
bang	瀏海	
fringe	短瀏海	
short hair	短髮	
long hair	長髮	
medium long hair	中長髮	
curly	捲髮	
wavy bouncy	微捲	
soft wave	自然大波浪捲髮	
straight	直髮	
ponytail	馬尾	
afro	米粉頭	
bob	齊耳短髮	
braid	辮子	
pigtail		
bun	髮髻	
bald head	禿頭	
baldness		

其他

hairdresser	美髮師
hairdressing	理髮業

● 臉部

保養品名稱，作用及外觀

acne spot	青春痘療效
clean- purify-	清潔用
hydra-	保濕用
anti-	抗… 防…
alcohol-free	無酒精
multi-	多元
solvent	溶解
repair	修護
revitalize	活化
nutritious	滋養
gentle	溫和的
anti-wrinkle	抗老防皺
balancing	平衡酸鹼

清潔用品外觀

foam	泡沫式
milk	乳狀
cream	霜狀
gel	膠狀 透明

膚質及基礎保養

oily	油性膚質
dry	乾性膚質
normal	中性膚質
combination	混合性膚質
sensitive	敏感型膚質
toner **freshener**	化妝水
lotion	化妝水 凝露
gentle tonic	溫和化妝水
astringent	收斂水
firming lotion	緊膚水
smoothing tone	柔膚水
essence	精華液
moisturizer	保濕霜
cream	霜
moisturizer cream	護膚霜
day cream	日霜
night cream	晚霜
eye gel	眼部保養凝膠
lip balm	護唇膏
lip care	護唇用
facial mist **facile spray** **complexion mist**	臉部保濕噴霧

加強保養

eye mask	眼膜
mask facial mask masque pack	面膜
peeling	剝落式面膜
facial	作臉
lymphatic drainage	淋巴引流排毒

清潔用品

face wash	洗面乳
facial cleanser	臉部清潔
remover	卸妝露
makeup remover	卸裝水
makeup removing lotion	
	卸裝乳
deep cleanser	深層清潔
pore cleanser pore refining	毛孔清潔
nose cleansing strip	
	妙鼻貼 一種用於清潔鼻 頭粉刺的貼布
exfoliate	去角質
scrub	磨砂膏

彩妝打底

make up base	妝前霜 (021)
	飾底乳
	隔離霜
foundation	隔離霜
	粉底
liquid foundation	粉底液
	(通常較服貼)
stick	粉條
stick foundation	條狀粉底
	(通常質地偏乾，遮瑕力也較好)
2-way cake powder foundation	
	兩用粉餅
	(可乾濕兩用的粉餅)
mousse foundation	慕絲狀粉底
concealer	遮瑕膏
pressed power	粉餅
lucidity	蜜粉
loose powder	
powder	粉底
	蜜粉

眼部彩妝

eyeliner	眼線
	眼線筆

liquid eye liner	眼線液
eye shadow	眼影
mascara	睫毛膏
false eye lash	假睫毛
brow powder	眉粉
brow pencil	眉筆
waterproof	防水

修容

shading powder	修容餅
blush color blush	腮紅
shimmering powder	亮粉
glitter	亮片

唇部彩妝

lip liner	唇線筆
lip gloss	唇彩
lip color lipstick	口紅
long last lipstick	持久性口紅
lip coat	口紅保護膜

彩妝及保養工具

accessory	彩妝工具	(022)
applicator	刷具	
pencil sharpener	削筆器	
brush	刷子	
eye brush	眼影刷	
brow brush	眉刷	
lash curler	睫毛夾	
electric lash curler	燙睫毛器	
brow template	畫眉器	
blush brush	腮紅刷	
lip brush	口紅刷	
puff	粉撲	
sponge	海綿	
facial tissue **tissue**	面紙	
Kleenex	可麗舒，面紙 (品牌名稱延伸為面 紙通稱)	
oil absorbing sheet	吸油面紙	
cotton pad	化妝棉	
cotton bud **Q-tip**	棉花棒 棉花棒 品牌名稱，延伸為 棉花棒通稱	
shaver **razor**	刮刀，刮鬍刀	

● 身體

身體保養

body wash	沐浴精
body shampoo	
body lotion	身體潤膚露
body moisturizer	身體保濕
exfoliate	去角質
scrub	磨砂膏

身體除毛

hair removal	除毛
depilate	脫毛
shaving	刮毛
waxing	熱蠟除毛
tweeze	以鉗子拔除毛髮
tweezers	鑷子，拔毛鉗
laser hair removal	雷射除毛
ingrown hair	毛髮內生
bikini waxlng	比基尼線除毛
eyebrow shaping	修眉
hairy	多毛的，毛茸茸的
body hair	體毛
armpit hair	腋毛
lip hair	嘴唇上的細毛
belly hair	肚臍下的毛
leg hair	腿毛
pubic hair	陰毛

皮膚防曬

sun block	防曬用品	(023)
sun screen		
tanning lotion	助曬劑	
dark tan oil		
after sun	日曬後用品	
whitening	美白	
tan	曬成棕色	
bronze	曬黑	
	曬成古銅色	
skin bronzed	皮膚曬黑	
self tanning room	助曬機	
	不用外出曬太陽也	
	可以曬的很均勻	

形容外表

beautiful	美麗的
pretty	漂亮的
attractive	有吸引力的
charming	迷人的
cute	可愛的
good-looking	好看的
handsome	英俊的

形容各種體型

big	個頭很大
small	個頭小
beer belly	啤酒肚
overweight	超重的
fat	肥胖的
baby fat	嬰兒肥
chubby	豐滿 胖嘟嘟
thin	瘦瘦的
skinny	瘦的
slim	苗條
slender	修長苗條的
fit	體型剛好
tall	高的
short	矮的
ugly	醜的
heavy	重的
physique	體格，體型 多談男人的身材
figure	身材 多談女人的身材
macho **big** **muscular**	肌肉發達
curvy figure **stacked**	曲線玲瓏

指甲保養

manicure	修手指甲	(024)
pedicure	修腳趾甲	
hand lotion	護手霜	
hand moisturizer		
nail care	護甲油	
nail saver	護甲液	
nail color	指甲油	
nail enamel	亮光指甲油	
nail polish		
top coat	表層護甲液	
base coat	底層護甲油	
nail polish remover	去光水	
quick dry	快乾	
nail art	指甲藝術	
	指甲彩繪	
nail art design	指甲彩繪設計	
artificial nail	水晶指甲	
	人工指甲	
French manicure	法式美甲	
French nail	法式美甲彩繪	

整片指甲先上一層透明指甲油，然後在指甲
尖端塗一層白邊的美甲設計

● 整型減肥

體重評估

weight	體重
overweight	過重
underweight	過輕
goal weight	目標體重
obesity	過胖

減肥方式

diet dieting slim weight loss	節食
diet pill diet	減肥藥
meal replacement	代餐
artificial sweetener	代糖
physical activity	運動
fitness	健身
weight loss surgery bariatrics surgery obesity surgery	減肥手術

減肥評估

malnutrition	營養
nutritionist dietitian	營養師
energy imbalance	熱量失衡

recommended dietary	建議飲食	(025)
nutritional value	營養價值	
assessment	評估	
diet	飲食，膳食	

膳食

high fiber diet	高纖維飲食
low cholesterol diet	低膽固醇飲食
reducing diet	減肥飲食
therapeutic diet	治療性飲食
low fat diet	低脂飲食
BMI; body-mass-index	
	身體質量指數
BIA; bio-electrical impedance	
	體脂肪
BMR; basal metabolic rate	
	基礎代謝率
waist	腰圍
WHR; waist-hip ratio	腰臀比

整型相關單字

self-esteem	自信
carry out	完成，執行
celeb, celebrity	藝人，名人
vanity	虛榮心
go under the knife have surgery	動手術

put pressure on	使...感到壓力
iron out	燙平
natural looks	天生樣貌
abnormal	不正常的
artificial	人工
de-wrinkled	消除皺紋
fake	假的
cosmetic surgery **plastic surgery** **plastic aesthetic surgery**	美容整形手術
plastic surgeon	整形外科醫生
ops, operations	手術
collagen	膠原蛋白
botox **botulinum toxin**	肉毒桿菌
hyaluronic acid	玻尿酸，簡稱 HA
placenta extract	胎盤素
liposuction	抽脂
breasts reconstruction	乳房重建
breasts augmentation	乳房增大術
breasts reduction	乳房縮小術
breasts deformity	乳房矯正術
breast surgery **breast implant** **breast enlargement**	隆胸手術

silicon	矽膠	(026)
saline bag	生理食鹽水袋	
eyelid surgery	割雙眼皮	
augmentation rhinoplasty	隆鼻	
rhinoplasty nose job	整鼻手術	
butt implants	豐臀	
jaw implant	隆下巴	
bellybutton surgery	肚臍美容	
vaginal reconstruction	陰道重建手術	
scar revision	除疤痕	
nevus	除痣	
mole	痣	
laser treatment	雷射美容治療	
dermabrasion	磨皮	
facelift	拉皮	
micro facelift	局部拉皮	

● 逛街購物

相關用詞

boutique	精品店
souvenir shop	紀念品專賣店
duty-free shop	免稅商店

duty-free goods	免稅商品
super market	超級市場
flea market	跳蚤市場

賣場設備

aisle	走道
cart trolley	手推車
basket	籃子
section	區域
shelf	置物架
checkout counter	結帳櫃台
counter	櫃台

貨品版本及庫存

new arrival	新款
best seller	暢銷
out of print	絕版(書籍)
edition	版本
new edition	新版
out of stock	缺貨
in stock	有貨

折扣標示

one price only	不二價
10%off	打九折
20%off	打八折
30%off	打七折

40%off	打六折	(027)
50%off	打五折	
60%off	打四折	
70%off	打三折	
80%off	打兩折	
90%off	打一折	
free of charge	免費	
special offer	特價	
selected items	部分商品	
with this coupon	憑此優待券	
great sales	大拍賣	
on sale	拍賣	
sale	大減價	
half price sale	半價拍賣	
buy two get one free	買二送一	
trade in	折價換新	
clearance	出清存貨	
discount	打折扣	

尺寸標示

What size do you take?	你的尺碼多大？
What size are you?	你的尺碼多大？
I am a size 8	我穿八號。
L; Large size	大號
M; Medium size	中號
S; Small size	小號

| XL; Extra large | 特大號 |
| XS; Extra small | 特小號 |

付帳

pay	付款
I will take it.	這件我要了
pay in cash	付現
credit card	信用卡
accept credit card	接受信用卡
cash only	只接受現金
tip	小費
service fee	服務費
change	零錢
	兌換
installment	分期付款
overcharge	索價過高
	過高的價錢
clerk	店員

討價還價

Cheaper?	便宜一點好嗎？
discount	折扣
special discount	特別優待
not on sale	不打折
better deal better price	更好的價錢
drop the price	降點價

bargain	討價還價	
a real bargain	真便宜	
negotiate	討價還價	
beyond my budget	超出我的預算	
price is fixed	不二價	
price tag	價格標籤	
store-wide sale	全面大減價	
big year-end sale	年終大減價	

退貨

out of order not work	壞了
return refund	退還，退款
compensation	賠償，報酬，津貼
exchange	退換，換貨
receipt	收據
no refund	概不退換

● 各類休閒活動

運動

snooker, billiard	撞球
ping-pong table-tennis	乒乓球
badminton	羽毛球
volleyball	排球
cricket	板球

squash	壁球
tennis	網球
baseball	棒球
softball	壘球
handball	手球
hockey	曲棍球
bowling	保齡球
golf	高爾夫球
snooker	英式古典撞球
billiard	美式的花式撞球
soccer	英式足球
rugby	英式橄欖球
football	足球 美式足球
basketball	籃球
swim	游泳
breaststroke	蛙式
backstroke	仰式
freestyle	自由式
butterfly stroke	蝶式
roller skating	滑輪
inline skating	溜直排輪
skating	滑冰
skiing	滑雪
ski board	滑雪板
boxing	拳擊
karate	空手道

陸上休閒活動

climbing	爬山	(029)
camping	露營	
cycling	騎腳踏車	
kite	風箏	
fly a kite	放風箏	
riding	騎馬	
bungee jumping	高空彈跳	

空中休閒活動

aerial excursion	空中鳥瞰
parachute	降落傘 跳傘
balloon	熱氣球
helicopter	直昇機
glide	乘滑翔機飛行
glider	滑翔機
hang-glider	滑翔翼

水上休閒活動

scuba diving	潛水
diving	潛水，跳水
snorkeling	浮潛
surfing	衝浪
wake boarding	風浪板
water skiing	滑水
jet ski	水上摩托車

parasailing	拖曳傘
catamaran sailing	雙體船
windsurfing	風帆
sailing	帆船 航行
boating	遊艇 乘船遊玩
glass bottom boat	玻璃船
rowing	划船
banana boat	香蕉船
canoe	獨木舟
canoeing	划獨木舟
rafting	泛舟
island hopping	列島遊
cruise	巡航，出海
dolphin cruise	出海賞海豚
sunset cruise	出海賞夕陽
night fishing	夜釣
hire boat	包船

兒童休閒活動

marble	彈珠
kite	風箏
doll	娃娃
music box	音樂盒
teddy bear	玩具熊

tricycle	三輪車	(030)
puppet	木偶	
robot	機器人	
rocking horse	木馬	
seesaw	蹺蹺板	
swing	鞦韆	
slide	滑梯	
plastic model	塑膠模型	
remote control car	遙控汽車	
toy train	玩具火車	
dart	飛鏢	
yo-yo	溜溜球	
puzzle	拼圖	
windmill	風車	
toy	玩具	
toy bricks	積木	
slingshot	彈弓	
jump rope	跳繩	
merry-go-round	旋轉木馬	

賭場

blackjack	21 點
dealer	莊家
co-bank	合作坐莊
player	玩家
split	分牌

pocket card	底牌
club	梅花
diamond	方塊
heart	紅心
spade	黑桃
one pair	一對
two pairs	兩對
three of a kind	三同號 三條
straight	順子
flush	同花
full house	滿堂紅 葫蘆
four of a kind	四同號 四條 鐵枝
straight flush	同花順
royal flush	大同花順
super jackpot	超級大獎
scratch card	刮刮卡
small or big	賭大小
slot	老虎機
wheel	輪盤
roulette wheel	輪盤
bluff	虛張聲勢
wild card	萬能牌
sitting out	旁觀

		🎧031
straight bet	直注	
split bet	分注	
place bet	下注	
double down	加倍下注	
surrender	投降認賠	
shuffle	洗牌	
reshuffle	重新洗牌	
a deck	一副牌	
roll the dice.	擲骰子吧	
play cards	玩撲克牌	
don't cheat	不要作弊	
a higher poker hand	拿較大的牌	
change, please. chips, please.	請換籌碼	
The player wins.	玩家贏	
The deck is shuffled	洗好牌了	
Please place your bet.	請下注	
out of luck	運氣太差了	
lucky	幸運	

藝文

board game play chess	下棋
Weiqi the game of go	圍棋
chess	象棋

bridge	橋牌
cultural show	文化表演
live band music	樂團演奏
movie	電影欣賞
theater	戲劇
symphony	交響樂
classical music	古典音樂
solo	獨奏 獨唱
choir	合唱團 唱詩班
gallery	畫廊 美術館
exhibition	展覽
landscape	風景畫
still life	靜物畫
wash	淡水彩畫
brush drawing	毛筆畫
nude	裸體畫
Chinese painting	國畫
oil painting	油畫
watercolor	畫
pastel drawing	蠟筆畫
miniature	細密畫 微型畫
engraving	版畫

portrait	畫像	032
self-portrait	自畫像	
sculpture	雕塑學	
	雕刻	
sculptor	雕刻家	
artisan	工匠	
statue	人像	
	雕像	
figure	塑像	
bronze	銅像	
	青銅	
artist	大師	
	藝術家	
painter	畫家	
author	作者	

健身房設施

fitness equipment	健身器材
multi-function home gym	
	多功能運動器材
treadmill	跑步機
exercise bike fitness cycle	健身腳踏車
spin bike	飛輪健身車
rowing machine	划艇機
strength training bench	
	運動用長椅

tension training equipment	
	擴胸器
steppers	踏步機
moon walker	漫步機
elliptical trainer	登山機
pressure training equipment	
	壓力棒
bending bar	彎曲棒
bending spring	彎曲彈簧器
finger bar	手握器
combined training equipment	
	多功能拉力器
beauty salon	美容沙龍
sauna	三溫暖
steam bath	蒸氣浴
steam room	蒸氣房
health spa	健康 SPA

健身房休閒

gymnasium	健身房
fitness room	
warm up	暖身
exercise	運動，鍛鍊
work out	
walking	走路
jogging	慢跑
swimming	游泳
biking	騎腳踏車

push-up	伏地挺身	(033)
sit-up	仰臥起坐	
weightlifting	舉重	
aerobics	有氧舞蹈	
step aerobic	階梯有氧	

● 各種派對

派對小點心

pizza	比薩
waffle	鬆餅
muffin	鬆糕
biscuit	餅乾
cookie	
pancake	煎餅
juice	果汁
beer	啤酒
wine	酒
cake	蛋糕
sprinkle	撒在糕點上的糖粒
icing	糖衣，糖霜
frosting	

派對常見單字

organize a party	辦派對
throw a party	
artificial flower	人造花
blindfold	蒙眼布，眼罩

streamer	彩帶
banner	寫有標語的布條
balloon	氣球
confetti	五彩碎紙
face painting	彩繪臉譜

生日派對

birthday party	生日派對
birthday cake	生日蛋糕
slumber party pajama party	睡衣派對
sleepover	在朋友家過夜的派對，或指借住朋友家一晚
cake	蛋糕
present gift	禮物
wrapping paper	包裝紙
ribbon	絲帶
bow	蝴蝶結
candle	蠟燭
make a wish	許願
clown	小丑
magician	魔術師

告別單身派對

bachelor party	告別單身男子派對
bachelorette party	告別單身女子派對
wedding shower	
bridal shower	
stripper	脫衣舞孃 脫衣舞男

結婚派對

wedding party	結婚派對
marry	結婚
wedding cake	結婚蛋糕
maid of honor bridesmaid	伴娘
best man	伴郎
flower girl	花童
throw a bouquet	丟捧花
bride	新娘
groom	新郎
tuxedo	燕尾服
make a toast propose a toast	敬酒
Congratulations	恭禧
tie	領帶
bow tie	蝶形領結

聖誕跨年派對

Christmas party X'mas party	聖誕節
Christmas tree	聖誕樹
New Year's eve party	跨年派對
decorate	裝飾
ornament	裝飾品
X'mas carol	聖誕頌 聖誕歌曲
candy cane	枴杖糖
X'mas light	聖誕燈
illumination	燈會
lamp	燈泡
fireplace	火爐
reindeer	馴鹿
North Pole	北極
snowflake	雪花
celebrate	慶祝
mistletoe	檞寄生
wreath	花圈
sleigh	雪橇
Christmas lights	聖誕燈飾
star	星星
tinsel	金箔裝飾品
stocking	長襪
Bible	聖經

gingerbread man	薑餅娃娃	(035)
gingerbread house	薑餅屋	
snow	雪	
snowman	雪人	

新生兒派對

baby shower diaper shower baby sprinkle	新生兒派對，在新生兒出生前，由母親及朋友們開的派對。
diaper	尿布
pacifier	奶嘴
baby carrier	嬰兒揹袋
disposable diaper	免洗尿布
stroller	嬰兒推車
milk bottle	奶瓶
highchair	高腳椅
baby wipe	濕紙巾
crawl	爬行
bib	圍兜
teddy bear	泰迪熊

其他派對

house warming kitchen shower	新居落成派對
karaoke	卡啦 OK
farewell party	歡送會
coming of age	成年禮

superbowl party	超級盃派對
theme party	主題派對
masquerade	化裝舞會
costume party	化妝派對
poolside party	池邊派對
potluck	每人帶一道菜的聚餐派對
BBQ party	烤肉派對
tailgate party **tailgating picnic**	車尾野餐會
cocktail party	雞尾酒會
banquet	酒席 筵席
buffet party	自助餐會
fashion party	時尚派對
homecoming party	美國高中一年一度的校際舞會,多半在暑假後。
prom **senior prom**	舞會,畢業舞會
prom queen	舞會中最美的女孩
prom king	舞會中最帥的男孩
campus queen	校花
open house	開放自由參觀日

生活常識I

命理占星
生活用語
生活空間
文具用品
親屬稱謂
廚房用具及餐具
其他生活用具
浴室及急救箱
色彩

● 命理占星

占星

What's your sign?	你的星座是什麼？
character	特質
astrology	占星術
horoscope	占星術
zodiac	星座 黃道帶
twelve signs	十二星座
fire sign	火向星座
wind slgn	風向星座
earth sign	土向星座
water sign	水向星座

白羊座

Arise	白羊座
ambitious	有雄心的 野心勃勃的
persist	堅持
pure	純潔
sincere	真誠

金牛座

Taurus	金牛座
clean definition	愛恨分明
enthusiastic	熱心
kind heart	愛心

雙子座

Gemini	雙子座	
sociable	善交際
passionate	多情
unstable	不穩定
clever	聰明
promote	推銷
unpredictable	不可預料的

巨蟹座

Cancer	巨蟹座
motherly love	母愛
family	家庭
defensive	自衛性
romantic	浪漫
sensible	感性
sensitive	敏感 敏銳
picky	吹毛求疵 挑剔
fantasize	幻想
guardian	守護

獅子座

Leo	獅子座
show off	愛表現
passionate	熱情
career	事業

charisma	非凡的領導力
leadership	領導才能，統御力
aggressive	積極 侵略的
acting talent	表演天份
creativity	創造力
self-image	自我形象
self-esteem	自尊心

處女座

Virgo	處女座
sensitive	敏感
cautious	小心
perfection	完美
paranoid	偏執狂，神經質
reluctant	不情願
surrender	投降
calculate	計算
criticism	批評
number	數字
analytical	分析的
financial	金融的

天秤座

Libra	天秤座
fairness	公正
equalization	平等化
motto	座右銘

justice	正義	(038)
righteous	正直的 公正的	
peace	和平	
elegance	優雅	

天蠍座

Scorpio	天蠍座
conservative	保守
reserved	沈默寡言的 深沉的
mysterious	神秘感
confident	自信
energetic	精力旺盛
sexually active	性慾強烈

射手座

Sagittarius	人馬座 射手座
active power	行動力
agitated	激動的

魔羯座

Capricorn	山羊座 魔羯座
hard work	工作認真
mild temper	脾氣溫和
humbleness	謙遜
stable	沉穩

proclaim	讚揚 稱頌

水瓶座

Aquarius	水瓶座
freedom	自由
smart	聰明
sophisticated	老於世故的
strong ego	主觀意識強

雙魚座

Pieces	雙魚座
mild temper	脾氣溫和
easy going	隨和
generous	慷慨
kind	善良
quick thinker	反應靈敏的人

十二生肖

What animal sign were you born under?	你屬什麼？
rat	鼠
ox	牛
tiger	虎
rabbit	兔
dragon	龍
snake	蛇
horse	馬

sheep lamb	羊	(039)
monkey	猴	
rooster chicken	雞	
dog	狗	
pig boar	豬	

塔羅牌

Wands	權杖
Ace of Wands	權杖一
Two of Wands	權杖二
Cups	聖杯
Swords	寶劍
Pentacles	五角星
Fool	愚者
Magician	魔術師
High Priestess	女祭司
Empress	女皇
Emperor	國王
Hierophant	教皇
Lovers	情人
Chariot	戰車
Strength	力量
Hermit	隱士
Wheel of Fortune	命運之輪
Justice	正義

Hanged Man	倒吊人
Death	死亡
Temperance	節制
Devil	魔鬼
Tower	塔
Star	星星
Moon	月亮
Sun	太陽
Judgment	審判
World	世界

命理

fortune telling	算命
fortune teller	算命師
feng shui	風水
Chinese astrology	紫微斗數
palm reading	手相
face reading	面相
superstition	迷信
Tarot cards	塔羅牌
Twelve Years of Animals	十二生肖
twelve zodiac signs	十二星座
gain good luck	增加運勢
tell your future	測知你的未來
accurate	準確

● 生活用語

時間

time	時間	(040)
yesterday	昨天	
now	現在	
today	今天	
tonight	今晚	
tomorrow	明天	
morning	早晨	
day	白天	
noon	中午	
afternoon	下午	
evening	傍晚	
eve	前夕	
night	夜晚	
midnight	午夜	
future	未來	
hour	小時	
minute	分鐘	
second	秒	
moment	片刻	
date	日期	
month	月份	
season	季節	
year	年	

特殊節日

anniversary	週年紀念日
memorial day	紀念日
national holiday	國定假日
public holiday	
legal holiday	
commemorative holiday	
statutory holiday	
bank holiday	
holiday	假期
vacation	
festival	節慶，喜慶日

季節及氣候

spring	春
summer	夏
autumn, fall	秋
winter	冬
tropical zone	熱帶
subtropical zone	亞熱帶
temperate zone	溫帶
frigid zone	寒帶
monsoon zone	季風帶
oceanic climate	海洋性氣候
continental climate	大陸性氣候

氣候報導

the lows	最低氣溫	(041)
the highs	最高氣溫	
precipitation	降雨量	
fine fair sunny	晴朗	
mild warm	溫暖	
cool	涼爽	
hot	炎熱	
hot wave	熱浪	
cloudy	多雲	
clear to overcast	晴轉多雲	
cloudy to overcast	陰轉多雲	
turning out cloudy	轉陰	
overcast, dull, gloomy	陰天	
wet	雨天	
dew	露水	
drizzle	毛毛雨，小雨	
shower	陣雨	
thunder shower	雷陣雨	
pour, downpour	大雨	
storm	暴風雨	
thunder storm	雷雨	
seasonal rain	季節雨	
monsoon	季風，雨季	
sleet	雨夾雪	

thunder	打雷
lightning	閃電
snowy	有雪
light snow	小雪
blizzard	暴風雪
snowstorm	暴風雪
hail, hailstone	冰雹
avalanche	雪崩
ice storm	冰雹
windy	有風
breezy	微風陣陣
gentle wind	和風
gale	大風
heavy, high wind	大風
windy and dusty	風沙
gust	強陣風
foggy	有霧
frosty	霜凍
chilly	微冷
freezing	冰冷
frost	霜凍
misty	薄霧
dry	乾燥的
damp humid	潮濕的，有濕氣的
stuffy close	不通風的，悶熱的

氣候現象

global warming	全球暖化	(042)
greenhouse effect	溫室效應	
El Nino	聖嬰現象	
carbon dioxide	二氧化碳	
emit	排放	
global temperature	全球溫度	
rise	上升	

天然災害

dust storm	沙塵暴
tsunami	海嘯
typhoon	颱風
hurricane	颶風
tornado **twister**	龍捲風
flood	洪水
drought	旱災
earthquake	地震
landslide	山崩
mudslide	土石流
volcanic eruption	火山爆發
natural disaster	天然災害
calamity	災難
disaster-hit area	災區
death tolls	死亡人數，死亡率
casualty	遇難者，傷亡人員

● 生活空間

門、窗

front door	前門
back door	後門
door knob	門把
door lock	門鎖
window	窗戶
bay window	八角窗 向外凸出的窗戶
air window	氣窗
French door	落地門
screen	紗門，紗窗
aluminum door	鋁門窗
sliding glass door	玻璃拉門
door chain	門鏈
door bell	門鈴
window frame	窗框
windowsill	窗台
window pane	窗玻璃
window bar	窗閂
casement	向外推出的窗戶
valance	短的裝飾用窗簾
drape	落地窗簾
curtain	窗簾
blind	百葉窗簾
Venetian blind	活動百葉窗

室內外生活空間

entrance	玄關	(043)
bar	吧台	
living room	客廳	
fireplace	壁爐	
funnel	煙囪	
chimney Japanese room		
	和室	
mahjong room	麻將房	
kitchen	廚房	
bedroom	睡房	
main bedroom	主臥房	
master bedroom guest room		
	客房	
child room	小孩房	
bathroom	廁所	
restroom	廁所的委婉語	
shower	淋浴	
balcony	陽台	
porch	門廊，陽台	
attic	閣樓	
penthouse		
stairs	樓梯	
spiral staircase	螺旋梯	
basement	地下室	
cellar	地下室，酒窖	
dining room	飯廳	

study room	書房
laundry	洗衣間
walk-in closet	更衣間
parlor	起居室
storeroom	儲藏室
garage	車庫
garden	花園
back yard	後院
front yard	前院
drainage	排水系統
drainpipe	排水管
banisters	欄杆
cathedral ceiling	挑高天花板
ceiling	天花板
floor	地板
corridor	迴廊
hallway	
arcade	
aisl	
gallery	
entrance hall	穿堂
tunnel	隧道
panic room	
密室，尤其是古老豪宅內部才有的設計。	
chamber	
室，房間，單人的辦公室，(美)法官辦公室	

公共空間標語

for sale	吉屋出售	(044)
house for sale to let	吉屋出租	
for rent		
house for rent		
emergency exit	太平門	
lady's room	女廁所	
men's room	男廁所	
rest room	盥洗室	
ticket office	售票處	
telephone	電話	
no smoking	請勿吸煙	
do not touch	請勿觸摸	
no admittance	閒人勿進	
no visitors	謝絕參觀	
danger	危險	
dead end	此路不通	
wet paint	油漆未乾	
pull	拉	
push	推	
welcome	歡迎	
thanks for coming	謝謝光臨	
store hours	營業時間	
cross walk	行人穿越道	

房屋的種類

apartment	公寓
house	房子
flat	一層公寓
cottage	獨棟的屋子
en-suite	套房 房內有獨立的洗手間和淋浴間
shack	棚屋 簡陋的木屋
bungalow	平房，小屋
lodge	看守人的小屋 守衛室
suite	套房 共用洗手間及浴室
building	房屋建築物

● 文具用品

紙

paper	紙
notebook	筆記簿
notebook binder	筆記本活頁夾
loose-leaf book	活頁簿
binder	活頁封套
organizer	講義夾
folder	文件夾
post-it paper	浮貼便條紙

scrape paper	便條紙	🎧045
self-adhesive label	即貼標籤	
recycled paper	回收紙	
brown paper	牛皮紙	
carbon paper	複寫紙	
cardboard	厚紙板	
wrapping paper	包裝紙	

黏著工具

duct tape thick tape wide tape	粗膠帶
thin tape	細膠帶
tape	膠帶
tape dispenser	膠帶台
glue	膠水，白膠
glue stick	口紅膠

筆

pencil	鉛筆
chalk a piece of chalk	粉筆 一支粉筆
mechanical pen	自動筆
mechanical pencil	自動鉛筆
pen	(鋼)筆
fountain pen	鋼筆
ball point pen ball pen	原子筆

highlighter	螢光筆
marker	麥克筆
	白板筆
	奇異筆
quill	鵝毛筆
calligraphy brush	毛筆
color pen	彩色筆
crayon	蠟筆
felt-tipped pen	彩色筆

文具

stationery	文具
	文具店
pencil box	鉛筆盒
dip	蘸濕(毛筆等)
ink	墨水
chop ink, seal ink	印泥
chop stamp	印章
seal stamp	
eraser	板擦，橡皮擦
rubber	
white out	修正液
correction fluid	
board	墊板
desk pad mat	
mouse pad	滑鼠墊
magnet	磁鐵
ruler	尺

		(046)
pen holder	筆筒	
(a pair of) scissors	(一把)剪刀	
utility knife	美工刀	
thumbtack	圖釘	
pin	大頭針	
safety pin	安全別針	
stapler	釘書機	
staple	釘書針	
clip **paper clip**	夾子，迴紋針	
sharpener **pencil sharpener**	削鉛筆機	
compass	圓規	
hole puncher	打洞機	
calculator	計算機	

其他用品

stop watch	馬錶
timer	計時器
rubber band	橡皮筋
dictionary	字典
phone book	電話簿
greeting card	賀卡
calendar	日曆 月曆
envelope	信封
paper box **cardboard box**	紙箱

card	名片
name card	
ID	識別證
identification	
name tag	名牌
sticker	貼紙
bookmark	書籤

● 親屬稱謂

親屬關係

great-grandparents	曾祖父母
grandparents	祖父母
grandfather	祖父
grandmother	祖母
father	父親
mother	母親
father-in-law	公公
mother-in-law	婆婆
husband	丈夫
wife	妻子
uncle	伯
	叔
	舅
	姑
	姨父

aunt	伯 (047)
	叔
	舅
	姑
	姨母
cousin	堂兄弟姊妹
	表兄弟姊妹
brother	兄弟
sister	姊妹
elder brother	哥哥
younger brother	弟弟
sister-in-law	嫂子
	弟妹
younger sister	妹妹
elder sister	姊姊
brother-in-law	姊夫
	妹夫
daughter	女兒
son-in-law	女婿
son	兒子
daughter-in-law	媳婦
nephew	侄子
niece	侄女
granddaughter	孫女
grandson	外孫子
child	小孩子
children	小孩子(複數)

● 廚房用具及餐具

筷子、叉子、湯匙、餐刀

dinner fork	餐叉
salad fork	沙拉叉
salad tongs	沙拉夾
two-pronged fork	大叉子
chopsticks	筷子
chopsticks rack	筷架
spoon	湯匙
teaspoon	茶匙
carving fork	大型餐刀
steak knife	牛排刀
knife	刀子
spatula	抹刀
utensil holder	刀具架

盤子

dish	深盤
plate	淺盤
platter	橢圓形大淺盤
saucer	醬碟 小碟子
tray	裝托盤
paper plate	紙盤

杯子，水壺

paper cup	紙杯	(048)
coffee cup	咖啡杯	
glass	玻璃杯	
stainless steel cup	鋼杯	
mug	馬克杯	
thermos cup	保溫杯	
wine glass	酒杯	
cup	茶杯	
champagne glass	香檳酒杯	
red wine glass	紅酒酒杯	
kettle	水壺	
jug	涼水壺	
teapot	茶壺	
coffeepot	咖啡壺	
pitcher	大水壺	

鍋具

pan	平底鍋
frying pan	煎鍋
cooker	鍋子
wok	中式炒鍋
pressure cooker	壓力鍋
griddle	煎餅的淺鍋
slow cooker	燉鍋
pot	湯鍋
skillet	煮鍋，有長柄的小鍋

廚房用具

peeler	削皮刀
paring knife	水果刀
cleaver **kitchen knife**	菜刀
pizza cutter	比薩刀
chopping board	砧板
cutting board	切菜板
sharpening steel	磨刀鋼條
draining spoon	漏匙
skimmer	漏勺
filter	濾器
funnel	漏斗
spatula	抹刀 刮鏟
turner	鍋鏟
ladle	長柄杓
ice cream scoop	挖冰淇淋器具
wooden spatula	木製飯杓
frying spoon	炒菜勺

塑膠袋、鋁箔紙

plastic bag	塑膠袋
paper bag	紙袋
trash bag	垃圾袋
doggie bag	打包袋
foil **aluminum foil**	鋁箔紙

保鮮膜、保鮮袋

cling film wax paper plastic wrap	保鮮膜	(049)
freezer bag wrapper	保鮮袋	
Ziploc	保鮮袋 品牌名延伸	

廚房設備

sideboard cupboard	食具櫃
sink	流理台 水槽
dish drain	裝洗過碗盤的托盤
strainer	濾網
table cloth	桌布
oven mitt potholder	耐熱手套
ice cube tray	製冰盒
towel holder	紙巾架
kitchen towel	廚房紙巾

壓碎、攪拌器

electric mixer	攪拌器
grater	磨碎器 擦菜板
nutcracker	堅果鉗
grinter	磨碎器(咖啡)

whisk	攪拌器
blender mixer	果汁機
stirrer	飲料攪拌棒

其他

tableware utensil	餐具
silverware	銀器，多指餐具
straw	吸管
bowl	碗
napkin	餐巾
paper towel	紙巾
measure cup	量杯
measuring spoon	計量匙
kitchen scale	廚房小磅秤
bottle opener	開瓶器
can opener	開罐器
corkscrew	軟木塞拔，開酒器
rolling pln	桿麵棍

● 其他生活用具

洗衣，更衣間，衣物整理

do the laundry	洗衣
washer	洗衣機
dryer	乾衣機
dirty laundry	要洗的衣服

laundry basket	洗衣籃	(050)
soap	肥皂 洗衣粉	
softener	柔軟精	
detergent	洗衣粉，清潔劑	
vender machine	洗衣粉販賣機	
bleach	漂白水	
non-chlorine bleach	不含氯的漂白劑	
fabric softener	衣物柔軟精	
wash	洗衣	
rinse	沖滌	
spin	脫水	
hang laundry	晾衣服	
clothespin	衣夾	
coat rack	衣帽架	
hanger	衣架	
hat rack	帽架	
closet wardrobe	衣櫥	
fold	折(衣服)	
clothespin	衣夾	
hanger	衣架	
dry clean	乾洗	
laundry cleaner	洗衣店	
collect laundry	收集要洗的衣服	
wrinkle	(衣服)變皺	

iron	燙(衣服)
iron out the wrinkles	燙平
iron	熨斗
ironing board	燙衣板

臥房

pillow	枕頭
sheet	床單
bedspread	床罩
blanket	毛毯
quilt	厚被
mattress	彈簧床
single bed	單人床
bunk bed	雙層床 多層床
night stand	床頭櫃

工具箱

toolbox	工具箱
hammer	榔頭，鐵鎚
nail	鐵釘
screw	螺絲釘
gimlet	螺絲錐
nail puller	拔釘器
screwdriver	螺絲起子
spanner	扳手，螺旋鉗
tape measure	皮尺
soldering iron	焊接棒

nipper	鑷子	(051)
pliers	鉗子	
ax	斧頭	
shovel	鏟子	
chisel	鑿子	
spade	鏟，鍬	
hoe	鋤頭	
pick	十字鎬	
pitch fork	草耙	
plane	鉋子	
saw file	銼刀	
reaping-hook	鐮刀	
rake	耙子	
scythe	大鐮刀	
tape	膠帶	
ladder	梯子	
electric drill	電鑽	
saw	鋸子	
electric saw	電鋸	
pit saw	雙人用的大鋸	
bucket	水桶	
rope	繩索	
paint	油漆	
paintbrush	油漆刷	
brush	刷子	
paint roller	油漆滾筒	
trowel	水泥刀	

其他

rack	架子
ashtray	煙灰缸
hamper	有蓋的籃子 洗衣籃
plywood	合板，三夾板
tapestry	掛畫，掛氈
tile	磁磚
wallpaper	壁紙
rug	地毯
wall-to-wall carpet	全鋪地毯
key	鑰匙
fuse	保險絲
globe	地球儀
match	火柴
lighter	打火機

環境清潔用品

detergent	洗潔精，沙拉脫
broom	掃帚
dustpan	畚箕
mop	拖把
duster	雞毛撢子
flyswatter	蒼蠅拍
pesticide bug spray	殺蟲劑
insect repellent	用於戶外的防蟲劑

dust cloth	抹布	(052)
rag	較髒破的抹布	
deodorant	芳香劑	
desiccant	乾燥劑	
mothballs	樟腦丸	
glass cleaner	玻璃清潔劑	
scouring pad	菜瓜布	
bucket	水桶	
dipper	水瓢	

電器及傢俱

radio	收音機
air freshener	空氣清淨機
VCR Video Cassette Recorder	錄放影機
CD player	CD 播放器
electric radiator heater	暖爐
TV set	電視機
washing machine	洗衣機
electric fan	電扇
vacuum cleaner cleaner vacuum	吸塵器
thermos	熱水瓶
water heater	熱水器
air-conditioner	冷氣

central air conditioner	中央空調
stereo set	音響組合
microwave oven	微波爐
oven	烤箱
grill	烤架
roaster	烤爐
toaster	烤麵包機
coffee maker	咖啡壺
electric coffee pot	電咖啡壺
percolator	過濾式咖啡壺
coffee filter	濾紙
dish washer	洗碗機
dish dryer	烘碗機
electric cooker	電子鍋
rice cooker	電鍋
stove	火爐
fridge	冰箱
refrigerator	冷藏室
freezer	冷凍室
ceiling fan	吊扇
light	燈
lamp	有罩燈
desk lamp **table lamp**	桌燈
clip lamp	夾燈
table lamp	檯燈

light bulb	燈泡	(053)
filament	燈絲	
candle	蠟燭	
flashlight	手電筒	
desk	書桌 辦公桌	
table	桌子	
dining table	餐桌	
picnic table	野餐桌	
coffee table	大茶几 客廳沙發前的矮桌	
end table	小茶几	
cocktail table	茶几	
folding table	摺疊桌	
dressing table vanity	梳妝台	
worktable	工作台，縫紉台	
recliner	坐臥兩用椅	
sofa couch	沙發	
cushion	椅墊	
love seat	雙人沙發	
lounge chair	休閒椅	
couch	長沙發，貴妃椅	
fabric chair	塑膠椅	
bar stool	高腳椅	
high chair	兒童椅	

rocking chair armchair	搖椅
stool	凳子
steel chair	鐵椅
wood chair	木椅
bookcase	書櫃
bureau	臥房用衣櫃
chest	五斗櫃
drawer	抽屜
night table night stand	床頭櫃

● 浴室及急救箱

浴室設備

showerhead	蓮蓬頭
faucet, tap	水龍頭
bathtub	浴缸
towel rack	毛巾架
mirror	鏡子
toilet	馬桶
water tank	水箱
shower curtain	浴簾
dryer	吹風機
ventilator fan	抽風機

tissue	面紙，衛生紙 (054)
facial tissue	
tissue paper	
toilet paper	
Kleenex	衛生紙，品牌名延用為常用字
garbage can	垃圾桶
trash can	
towel	毛巾
shower cap	浴帽

身體清潔用品

soap	肥皂
soap dish	肥皂盒
soap container	
bath foam	沐浴乳
shampoo	洗髮精
conditioner	潤絲精
mouth wash	漱口水
toothpick	牙籤
toothpaste	牙膏
toothbrush	牙刷
dental floss	牙線
shaver	電動刮鬍刀
razor	一般刮鬍刀
blade	刮鬍刀的刀片
nose hair clippers	鼻毛剪
nail clippers	指甲刀

nail file	指甲銼
ear pick	耳挖
cotton swab	棉花棒
Q Tip	棉花棒，品牌名延伸為常用字
pumice	磨腳石

急救箱

alcohol prep pad	藥用酒精片
75% alcohol	藥用酒精
povidone-iodine prep pad	碘酒藥片
mercurochrome solution	紅藥水(商標名)
hydrogen peroxide solution	雙氧水
ointment	軟膏
ice pack	冰枕
ice bag	冰袋
tongs	鑷子
scissors	剪刀
thermometer	温度計
cotton ball	棉花球
surgical tape	透氣膠帶
tourniquet	止血帶
bandage	繃帶
Band-Aid	OK 繃
adhesive tape	膠帶

first aid kit	急救箱	(055)
medicine cabinet	醫藥櫃	
painkiller	止痛藥	
Aspirin	阿斯匹靈	
digestive	消化藥	
cough syrup	止咳糖漿	
sleeping potion	安眠藥	
sleeping pill		
vitamin	維他命	
Centrum	善存片	
	綜合維他命品牌名	
aline	生理食鹽水	
saline solution		
cravat	三角巾	
scarf bandage		
gauze	紗布	
sanitary glove	衛生手套	
surgical mask	手術口罩	
tongue blades	壓舌板	
spatula		
forceps	鑷子	
tourniquet	止血帶	
tray	托盤	
needle	針頭	

● 色彩

米黃色系列

camel	駝色
amber	琥珀色
khaki	卡其色
maroon	褐紅色
chestnut	栗色
corn silk	米綢色
tan	茶色
yellow	黃色
yellow green chartreuse	黃綠色

綠色系列

cadet blue	軍藍色
moss green	苔綠色
emerald green	鮮綠色
olive	橄欖色
olive drab	深綠褐色
pale green	淡綠色
olive green	橄欖綠
cyan	青綠色
mint cream	薄荷色
sea green	海綠色
teal	藍綠色
turquoise	青綠色
turquoise blue	翠藍色

灰色系列

gray	灰色	(056)
charcoal gray	炭灰色	
smoky gray	煙灰色	
misty gray	霧灰色	
taupe	褐灰色	
ecru	淺灰黃，亞麻色	

藍色系列

blue	藍色
blue violet	紫羅蘭色
cornflower blue	菊藍色
sapphire	寶石藍
turquoise blue	土耳其玉色
cobalt blue	鈷藍色
	豔藍色
navy blue	藏青色
	深藍色
powder blue	粉藍色
royal blue	寶藍色
sky blue	天藍色
azure	青灰色
	石藍色
slate blue	石藍色
steel blue	鋼藍色
aquamarine	藍綠色
	海藍色
aqua	淺藍色

紫色系列

purple	紫色
violet	
lavender	淡紫色
orchid	
lilac	
antique violet	古紫色
pale violet red	淡紫羅藍色
pansy	紫羅蘭色

白色系列

white	白色
blanched almond	白杏色
antique white	古董白
off-white	灰白色
Navajo white	納瓦白
seashell	海貝色
ivory	象牙色
snowy white	雪白色
oyster white	乳白色
wheat	小麥色

紅褐色系列

red	紅色
scarlet	緋紅 猩紅
peach	桃色
pink	粉紅

plum	梅子色	(057)
mauve	紫紅	
wine red	葡萄酒紅	
ruby	寶石紅	
pink	粉紅色	
misty rose	淺玫瑰色	
salmon pink	橙紅色	
baby pink	淺粉紅色	
shocking pink	鮮粉紅色	
orange	橙色	
orange red	橙紅色	
rosy brown	褐玫瑰紅	
coral	珊瑚色	
crimson	暗深紅色	
magenta	洋紅色	
sienna	赭色	
brown	褐色 茶色	
burly wood	實木色	
chocolate	巧克力色	
moccasin	鹿皮色	
beige	米色 灰褐色	
chocolate	紅褐色 赭石色	
sandy beige	淺褐色	
saddle brown	重褐色	
sandy brown	沙褐色	

其他顏色

color	色彩
black	黑色
silver	銀白色
gold	金色

生活常識 Ⅱ

● 常用符號

溫度符號

| Celsius | 攝式(℃) | |
| Fahrenheit | 華式(℉) | |

標點符號

punctuation mark	標點符號
comma	逗號(，)
period	句號(。, .)
full stop	句號(。, .)
exclamation mark	驚嘆號(！)
colon	冒號(：)
semicolon	分號(，)
parenthesis	括號( ) [ ] { }
brackets	
question mark	問號(？)
slash	斜線 (／)
dot	點(.)
dash	破折號(-)
quotation mark	引號(" ")
hyphen	連字號(-)
apostrophe	省略號
	所有格符號(')
abbreviation	縮寫，略語

數字運算符號

operator	運算符號	(059)
plus add	加(+)	
minus subtract	減(−)	
multiply times	乘(×, *)	
divide	除(÷, /)	
square root	平方根(√)	
root extraction evolution extraction	開方	
square root	二次方根 平方根	
cube root	三次方根 立方根($_3\sqrt{}$)	
the root of four the fourth root	四次方根($_4\sqrt{}$)	
the root of n the n_{th} root	N 次方根($_n\sqrt{}$)	
power	次方	
square	二次方 平方(a_2)	
cube	三次方 立方(a_3)	
the power of four the fourth power	四次方(a_4)	

the power of n	N 次方(a_n)
the n_{th} power	
is equal to	等於（＝）
is not equal to	不等於（≠）
is greater than	大於（＞）
is lesser than	小於（＜）
is equal or greater than	
	大於等於（≥）
is equal or lesser than	
	小於等於（≤）
ratio	比（：）
proportion	比例（：, /）
percent	百分比（%）
function	函數（f(x)）
infinite	無窮大（∞）
infinitesimal	無窮小

● 數學運算

加	
addition	加法
augend	被加數
summand	
addend	加數
sum	和

減

subtraction	減法	(060)
minuend	被減數	
subtrahend	減數	
remainder	差	

乘

multiplication	乘法
multiplicand faciend	被乘數
multiplicator	乘數
product	積
power	次方
the power of n the nth power	N 次方
square	平方
cube	立方

除

division	除法
dividend	被除數
divisor	除數
quotient	商
to the nearest	最接近的
root	根號
the root of n the nth root	N 次方根

| square root | 平方根 |
| cube root | 立方根 |

其他運算

ratio	比例
matrix	矩陣
science notation	科學記號
limit	極限
standard deviation	標準差
average	平均數
weight	加權
weighted average	加權平均數
absolute value	絕對值

等於、不等於

total	總合，總計
amount	
(not) equal	(不)等於
is (not) equal to	
is (not) equivalent to	

大於、小於

range	值域
is greater than	大於
is lesser than	小於
is equal or greater than	大於等於
is equal of lesser than	小於等於

四捨五入

carry	進位	(061)
truncation	捨去	
round to round off	四捨五入	
round down	無條件捨去	
round up	無條件進位	
significant digit	(四捨五入) 有效數字	
insignificant digit	(四捨五入) 無效數字	

● 數字詞彙

數字

digit number	數字
null zero naught nil	零
integer	整數
positive	正數
negative	負數
odd number	單數，奇數
even number	雙數，偶數
cardinal number	基數 (指 one, two, three …)

ordinal number	序數 (指 first, second, third…)
natural number	自然數
factor	因數
prime	質數
function	函數

分數

fraction	分數
numerator	分子
denominator	分母

小數

decimal	小數
decimal point	小數點
decimal place	小數點右邊第一個數字
3 decimal places	小數點以下第三位

其他數字詞彙

mean	平均數
median	中位數
mode	眾數
real number	實數
variable	變數
binary system	二進位
decimal system	十進位
hexadecimal system	十六進位

● 幾何詞彙

點線(一維空間)

point	點	(062)
line	線	
parallel	平行線	
intersect	相交	

面積(二維空間)

plane	面
2-D **two-dimensional**	二維的
area	面積
length	長
width	寬
square	正方形
quadrilateral	四邊形
rectangle	長方形
diamond	菱形
parallelogram	平行四邊形
trapezoid	梯形
circle	圓
center	圓心
radius	半徑
diameter	直徑
pi	圓周率
circumference	圓周

semicircle	半圓
sector	扇形
ring	環
ellipse	橢圓
base	底
side	邊
height	高
triangle	三角形
angle	角
degree	角度
arc	弧

體積(三維空間)

cube	立方體
3-D, three-dimensional	三維的
space	空間
volume	體積
undersurface	底面
surface area	表面積
cone	圓錐
cylinder	圓柱
sphere	球
hemisphere	半球

商用圖表

data	資料
table	數字組成的圖表

graph	圖案組成的圖表 (063)
diagram	
chart	
plot	
pie chart	圓餅圖
flow chart	流程圖
bar chart	柱狀圖
histogram	長條圖
line chart	曲線圖
function	函數圖

● 常用單位及度量衡

長度	
kilometer	一公里
hectometer	公引
decameter	公丈
meter	公尺
decimeter	公寸
centimeter	公分
millimeter	公釐
yard	碼
foot	呎
inch	吋

一組、一套	
dozen	一打
gross	籮，十二打

set	組，套
dozen set	打 / 套
pair set	雙 / 套
dozen pairs	雙 / 打
lot	一堆，一批
kit	套，組
suit	一套，一副
stack	一堆，一疊
string	一串，一連 一列，一隊

面積

square decimeter	平方公寸
square centimeter	平方公分
square decimeter	平方公寸
square foot	平方呎
square inch	平方吋
square meter	平方公尺
square yard	平方碼

重量

kilogram	公斤
gram	公克
hectogram	公兩，百克
decagram	公錢，十公克
decigram	公銖(十分之一公克)
centigram milligram	毫克(千分之一克)

quintal	公擔	(064)
ounce	英兩，盎斯	
pound	磅	
kiloton	千公噸	
metric ton	公噸	
ton	噸	
metric carat	克拉(寶石單位)	
catty	斤(中國=600 克)	
picul	擔(100 斤)	

盤狀單位

skid	(移動重物用的)墊木，滑動墊木，件
pallet	墊板，金屬或木頭材質之低臺
lift	一次搬起或運起之量
disc, disk	盤
tray	盤，碟

圓柱狀

cask	桶
pail	
tank	
bucket	
drum	
barrel	桶 (石油)
vat	大桶
keg	小桶 容量小於十加侖

can	罐
tin	
jar	罐，瓶，壺
pot	
bottle	
vial	小坡璃瓶
tube	支，管，筒
cylinder	汽缸
	圓筒
cone	筒

體積

hectoliter	公石
liter	公升
deciliter	公合
centiliter	公勺
milliliter	公撮
kiloliter	公秉
deciliter, dekaliter	公斗
gallon	加侖
pint	品脫
quart	夸爾(液量單位)
cubic centimeter	立方公分
cubic decimeter	立方公寸
cubic foot	立方呎
cubic inch	立方吋
cubic meter	立方公尺

袋狀

bag	袋，包	(065)
bale	包，件，捆	
sachet	小袋	
packet	小包，捆	
envelop	包，袋，信封	
pack	包，綑，副，組	
parcel	包，裹	
package	件，包	
poly bag	塑膠袋	

箱狀單位

cartridge	匣
chest	箱，匣
case	箱，盒
casket	(放貴重物品的) 小盒子 首飾盒
carton	(紙)箱
box	箱
van pack	包裝箱數量單位
wooden case	木箱
van	件 (大木箱)
container	罐，箱 容器，貨櫃
crate	板條箱

以交通工具為單位

vessel	艘(船)
unit	部，輛 (車輛)
container bulk cargo	散裝貨櫃
liquid bulk	(液體貨物) 散裝櫃

其他單位

each	每個
piece	個，片，塊
bulk	堆，散裝量
copy	冊，本
dose	一劑
sheet	張，片
segment	節，片
capsule	膠囊，粒 顆(藥用)
block	塊
log	圓木
frame	框，架子，套
bunch	串，束
bundle	捆
belt	帶，條
spool	捲，軸
bobbin	線軸
stick	支

rod	支，竿 棒，桿	(066)
strip	片，條	
basket	籃	
reel	捲，軸	
ring	環，圈	
roll	捲	
volume	冊，卷	
coil	捲	
panel	板	
plate	板，片	
slab	厚板，厚片	
syringe	注射器	
rack	架(網架、槍架、 刀、帽子架等)	
tablet	錠，片	
ingot	錠，條 塊	
quire	刀(紙張數量單位)	
ream	令(紙張數量單位)	
curie	居禮 (放射能的單位)	
cut	亞麻等之長度單位 (三百碼)	
quarter	夸特	

● 各國宗教

宗教

religion	宗教 信仰
religious	虔誠的 信奉宗教的 宗教上的
Buddhism	佛教
Lamaism	喇嘛教
Taoism	道教
Islam	伊斯蘭教
Christianity	基督教
Catholicism	天主教
The Eastern Church **The Orthodox Church**	東正教
Greek Orthodox Church	希臘正教
Shamanism	薩滿教 黃教
Judaism	猶太教
Confucianism	儒教 孔教

宗教儀式

pray	禱告，祈禱
ceremony	儀式，典禮
donate	捐獻，奉獻

ritual	(宗教的)儀式	(067)
religious rite	宗教儀式	
baptism	洗禮	
receive baptism	受洗	
be baptized	受洗	
confession	懺悔	
religious service	宗教儀式，禮拜	
religious ceremony	宗教祭典	
worship	祭拜	
attend religious service		
	做禮拜	
go to church	做禮拜	
attend Mass	做彌撒	
Sunday-school Sabbath-school	主日學，星期日學校	
sermon	講道	
chant	聖歌，歌唱，吟誦	
meditate meditation	沈思，冥想	
ghost	鬼，鬼魂，幽靈	
spirit	靈，靈魂	

宗教器具

rosary prayer beads	念珠，佛珠
the Bible	聖經
Buddhist scriptures	佛經
the Koran	可蘭經
incense	香
burner	燈，爐
snuff	燈花，燭花
sedan	轎子
paper money	紙錢
lamp stand	燈台
lantern	燈籠
veil	幔子
altar of incense	香壇
incense burner	香爐
candle	蠟燭
altar	香案，祭壇
Holy Place	聖所
Holy of Holies	至聖所
donation box	奉獻箱，功德箱
shrine	神祠，神龕
ephod	猶太教大祭司所穿 的聖衣
firecrackers	鞭炮，爆竹
ash	骨灰，香灰

寺廟內景

holy	神聖的 聖潔的	(068)
sacred	宗教的 莊嚴的 神聖的	
splendid	燦爛的	
offering	祭品，供品	
tablet	匾額	
dragon	龍	
phoenix	鳳凰	
column pillar	圓柱，梁	
carving	雕刻品	
relief	浮雕	
eaves	屋簷 (常用複數型)	
decorate	裝飾	
decoration	牌匾 牆壁上作為裝飾或 紀念的金屬薄片或 瓷片	
ancestor	祖先，祖宗	
God	神明	
goddess	女神	
urn	骨灰罈	

宗教處所

seminary	神學院
temple	廟宇，寺(佛 / 道教)
lamasery	喇嘛廟
mosque	清真寺 (伊斯蘭教)
monastery	寺院 修道院
Buddhist nunnery	庵(佛教)
abbey	修道院
convent nunnery	女修道院
church	教堂(基督教)
cathedral	大教堂 (天主教)
altar	祭壇，聖壇 聖餐台
synagogue	猶太教堂

宗教人物

believer, follower	信徒
Buddhist	佛教徒
Living Buddha	活佛
Buddhist monk	和尚
lama	喇嘛
Buddhist nun	尼姑
Taoist priest	道士
Taoist nun	道姑
clergyman	教士，牧師

rabbi	猶太教祭司	(069)
Muslim, Moslem	穆斯林	
ahung, imam	阿訇(伊斯蘭教宗教領袖或學者的尊稱)	
Catholic	天主教徒	
Christian	基督教徒	
Pope **the Holy Father**	教皇(天主教)	
cardinal	紅衣主教(天主教)	
archbishop	大主教(天主 / 基督教)	
bishop	主教(天主 / 基督教)	
priest	神父(天主教)	
nun	修女(天主教)	
pastor, minister	牧師(基督教)	
high priest	大祭司	
confucianist	信奉儒教的人	
worshipper	參拜者，香客	

● 節日習俗

節慶單字

festival	節慶
holiday	假日
celebration	慶祝

感恩節

Thanksgiving Day	感恩節
Pilgrim	清教徒
Indian	印地安人
The Mayflower	五月花號船
turkey	火雞
mashed potato	馬鈴薯泥
corn	玉米
pumpkin pie	南瓜派

復活節

Easter Day **Easter Holiday**	復活節
Easter egg	復活節彩蛋
Easter bunny	兔子
flower	花朵
tree	樹木
bird	鳥
basket	籃子
Easter egg hunting	找蛋遊戲

情人節

St. Valentine's Day	情人節
chocolate	巧克力
flower	花
lover	愛人 情人
confession	告白

聖派翠克節

St. Patrick's Day	聖派翠克節	(070)
green	綠色	
shamrock	酢漿草	
Ireland	愛爾蘭	
Christian	基督教徒	
Christianity	基督教	

教師節

Teacher's Day	教師節
Confucius	孔子
respect	尊敬
make a thank you card	
	做一張感謝卡

萬聖節

Hallowmas	萬聖節，**11** 月 **1** 日
Halloween	萬聖節前夕
	西洋鬼節
Happy Halloween!	萬聖節快樂！
pumpkin	南瓜
jack-o-lantern	南瓜燈
costume	化妝服
costume parade	化妝舞會遊行
ghost	鬼
vampire	吸血鬼

scary	嚇人的
skeleton	骷髏
bat	蝙蝠
owl	貓頭鷹
goblin	小妖精
witch	巫婆
broom	掃帚
trick or treat	不給糖就搗蛋
knock	敲，敲門
princess	公主
pirate	海盜
mask	面具 面罩
haunted house	鬼屋探險

聖誕節

Christmas Day	耶誕節， 12 月 25 日
Merry Christmas!	聖誕節快樂！
Finland	芬蘭 (聖誕老公公的 故鄉)
Santa Claus	聖誕老人
reindeer	馴鹿
Rudolph	魯道夫(拉雪橇的 紅鼻子馴鹿)

sleigh	雪橇	(071)
elf	小精靈	
elves	小精靈(複數)	
present gift	禮物	
bulb	燈泡	
socks, stocking	長統襪	
gingerbread man	薑餅人	
candy cane	枴杖糖	
Christmas tree	耶誕樹	
Christmas card	耶誕卡片	
Christmas carol	聖歌 讚美詩	
Jesus	耶穌	
snow	雪	
poinsettia	聖誕紅	

春節

Spring Festival Chinese New Year lunar new year	春節,過年
lunar calendar	農曆
lunar January	正月
paper-cuts	剪紙
couplets	春聯
firecrackers	鞭炮
dumpling	元寶 水餃

rice cake	年糕
rice ball	湯圓
dragon dance	舞龍
fireworks	煙火
firecrackers	爆竹
red envelop	紅包
gift money	壓歲錢
lion dance	舞獅
dragon dance	舞龍
traditional opera	戲曲
variety show **vaudeville**	雜耍，綜藝秀
riddles written on lanterns	
	燈謎
exhibit of lanterns	燈會
staying-up	守歲
give New Year's greetings	
	拜年
taboo	禁忌
family reunion dinner	團圓飯
the dinner on New Year's Eve	
	年夜飯
rice pudding	八寶飯
candy tray	糖果盤
The Lantern Festival	元宵節
lantern	燈籠

中秋節

Moon Festival	中秋節 陰曆 8 月 15 日	(072)
moon cake	月餅	
pomelo	柚子	
full moon	滿月	

● 大眾運輸工具

陸運工具相關詞彙

waiting room	候車室
platform	月臺
express train	快車
track, rail	鐵軌
slow train	慢車
subway station	地鐵車站
get off / get on	下車 / 上車
conductor	售票員
stop; station	車站
traffic jam	交通擁擠
berth; roomette	臥舖
seat	座位
hard sleeper	硬臥
soft sleeper	軟臥
bus stop	公車站
bus terminal	公車終點站

海運工具相關詞彙

ferry	渡輪
pier	碼頭
on boat	船上
in port	靠岸
lounge	休息室
cabin	甲板
upper deck	上層甲板

空運工具相關詞彙

check in	登機手續
passport	護照
ticket	機票
window seat	靠窗座位
aisle seat	走道座位
middle seat	中間的座位
emergency exit	緊急出口
legroom	伸腳的空間
toilet lavatory	洗手間
economy class	經濟艙
first class	頭等艙
business class	商務艙
on schedule	準點
boarding pass	登機證

luggage claim slip	行李認領單	(073)
gate	登機門	
boarding gate		
connecting flight counter		
	轉機櫃檯	
scale	(行李)磅秤	
carry-on item	隨身行李	
check your luggage	行李託運	
terminal A	A 航站	
confirm the flight	確認航班	
make a flight reservation		
	預定機票	
pre-boarding announcement		
	登機前的廣播	
stewardess	女乘務員	
steward	男乘務員	
flight attendant	空服員	
fasten the seat belt	繫上安全帶	
pilot	駕駛員	
customs officer	海關官員	
passenger	乘客	
take off	起飛	
departure time	起飛時間	
arrival time	飛抵時間	
destination	目的地	

大眾運輸常用詞語

time table	車時刻表
return ticket	回程票
one way ticket	單程票
book a ticket	訂票
refund	退票
transfer change	換車
information desk	問訊處
delay	誤點
fare	票價
exact change	恕不找零
exhaust pipe	排氣管
rear door	後門
rear window	後車窗
side mirror	側視鏡
rear view mirror	後視鏡
trunk	行李箱
spare tire	備胎
steering wheel	方向盤
seat belt	安全帶
seat belt buckle	安全帶扣環
A/C; air conditioner	空調
dashboard	儀錶版
odometer	里程表
speedometer	速度表
fuel meter	油表

accelerator	油門	(074)
brake	剎車	
emergency brake	手剎車	
clutch	離合器	
gears gear shift	排檔	
automatic	自排	
stick shift manual	手排	

兩輪、三輪交通工具

bicycle bike	腳踏車
tricycle	三輪腳踏車
motorcycle	摩托車
motor tricycle	三輪摩托車
three-wheeler	三輪摩托車

四輪交通工具

car	汽車
sedan	轎車
two-door sedan	兩門轎車
four-door sedan	四門轎車
subcompact sedan	小型轎車
compact sedan	中型轎車
full-size sedan	大型轎車
hatchback	掀背式汽車
convertible	敞篷車，跑車

limo, limousine	豪華轎車
coupe	雙門小轎車
sports car	跑車
race	賽車
van	箱型車
minivan	小型轎車

公務車及相關詞彙

ambulance	救護車
fire truck	消防車
squad car patrol car	警車，巡邏車
flashing lights	警示燈
siren	警鈴
ladder	梯子
hose	水管

陸上載客工具

bus	公共汽車
motor coach, coach	長途客車
double-deck bus	雙層公共汽車
minibus	小巴
shuttle bus	短程交通車
taxi, cab	計程車
coach, car	火車車廂
train	火車
passenger train	載客火車

freight train	運貨列車	(075)
goods train		
subway	地下鐵(美)	
	地下道(英)	
underground	地下鐵(英)	
tube		

旅行車、拖車、卡車

SUV, sport utility vehicle	
	運動休旅車
RV, recreational vehicle	
	野營休旅車
motor home	活動房屋旅行車
station wagon	客貨兩用旅行車
shooting brake	客貨兩用旅行車
jeep	吉普車
truck	卡車，旅行車
wagon	卡車
trailer	拖車
pickup truck	小貨車(無車蓋)，貨卡
light lorry, lorry	小貨車(英式)
platform truck	平臺卡車
eighteen-wheeler	18 輪大卡車
heavy lorry, heavy truck	
	重型卡車

水上交通工具

ship	船
jet boat	噴射艇
vessel	船舶
cargo vessel	貨輪
cargo carrier	
cargo boat	
freighter	

空中交通工具

plane	飛機
airplane	
helicopter	直昇機
chopper	
copter	
jet	噴射機
jet plane	
shuttle	太空梭
aerospace plane	
space ship	
oeing	波音
Concord	協和
aircraft	飛行交通工具
airbus	空中客車
special plane	專機
rocket	火箭
spaceship	太空船
glider	滑翔機

passenger plane	客機	(076)
monoplane	單翼飛機	
hang-glider	滑翔翼	
light aircraft	輕型飛機	
ultralight	超輕型飛機	
fighter airdraft fighter attaccker fighter	戰鬥機	
bomber	轟炸機	

● 交通號誌標語

交通標誌

exit	高速公路出口
entrance	高速公路入口
diverted traffic	交叉路口
right junction	右交叉口
traffic circle	圓環
look right	向右看
pedestrian crossing	當心行人
signal ahead	注意號誌
construction	道路施工
no entry	禁止進入
no through traffic no through way	禁止通行
do not enter	禁止進入
no left turn	禁止左轉

no right turn	禁止右轉
no U-turn	禁止迴車
no bicycles	禁行自行車
no honking	禁按喇叭
no loitering	禁止逗留
no parking	不准停車
no stops	不准停留
do not stop	請勿逗留
pedestrian crossing	前有人行道
please drive carefully	請小心駕駛
road closed	此路封閉
slow	慢行
speed limit	速限
VIP car park	貴賓停車場
guest's car park	來客停車場
limited parking	停車位有限
parking lot parking area car park	停車場
parking permitted	允許停車
no parking	禁止停車
parking for taxis only	只准許出租停
please do not park	請不要停車
strictly no parking	嚴禁停車
hill	險降坡
slippery	路滑

merge	匝道會車	(077)
one way	單行道	
two-way traffic	雙向道	
detour	繞道行駛	
stop	停	
traffic light	紅綠燈	

標語常見詞彙

belongings	私人物品
elderly person	老人(博愛座)
handicapped person	殘疾人(博愛座)

women with children
攜有兒童的婦女(博愛座)

do not speak to the driver.
請勿與司機交談。

bus lane	公車專用道
bus stand	公車站牌
bus information	公車詢問處
bus loading	公車上車處
keep gateways clear	保持通道暢通
retain your ticket	保留車票
inspection	驗票
tourist service	遊客服務台
information help desk	詢問處
taxi loading	計程車上車處

taxi stand	計程車招呼站
toilet engaged	廁所有人
mind the gap	小心月臺階間隙
stand clear off the door	請勿站在門口
valid until...	有效期到…
passenger terminal	航站大廈
money exchange	外幣兌換處
post office	郵局
airport lounge	機場休息室
arrival	入境
arrival lobby	入境大廳
departure	出境
departure waiting lounge	出境休息廳
parking lot	停車場
transit lounge	過境室
entry and exit service	入出境服務站
exit out	出口
entrance in	入口
holding room	候機室
check in area	辦理登機區
customer lounge	旅客休息室

flight connection	轉機處	(078)
domestic flight	國內航班	
passport control	入境檢驗	
emergency exit	安全出口	
airport shuttle	機場班車	
queue here	在此排隊	
no smoking	禁止吸煙	
left baggage	行李寄放	
lost property	失物招領	
luggage pick up luggage reclaim baggage claim	行李	
reclaim belt	行李傳送帶	
baggage cart	行李推車	
check-in counter	旅客登機報到台	
customs information customs service	海關服務台	
payment of customs duty 　　　　　　　　海關課稅處		
quarantine	檢疫	
duty free shop	免稅商店	
gift shop	禮品店	
restaurant	餐廳	
snack bar	快餐冷飲	
flight kitchen	空中廚房	

aviation medical center	
	航空醫療中心

方向詞彙

east	東
south	南
west	西
north	北
left on your left	左 在你左邊
right on your right	右 在你右邊
straight on	往前直去
go straight ahead	直走
there	那兒
here	這兒
front	前方
back	後方
opposite	對面的
by next to beside	在…旁
fork	分岔
side	側旁
before	之前
after	之後
cross opposite	橫越

between	在…中間	(079)
across from	在…對面	
on the opposite sidw of xx **face xx**	在 **xx** 的正對面	
on the side ofxx	與 **xx** 同一邊	
in front of **before**	在…（之）前	
in back of **behind**	在…（之）後	
around the corner from ...	在…的轉角	
on the corner of A and B	在 **A** 和 **B** 轉角	
on the main road	在主要道路上	
at the end of the street	在這條路尾/路頭	
block	街區 街廓	
close to	靠近	

迷路，無家可歸

lost **lose one's way** **get lost**	迷路
stray **stray from the path**	迷路，走失
long-lost	失蹤很久的

180

| **homeless** | 無家可歸 |
| | 漂泊遊蕩 |

問路

Excuse me.	請問一下
	打斷一下
	抱歉

| **Where is xx?** | xx 在哪兒? |

How do I get to xx?

Where is the nearest xxX?
離這裡最近的 xx 在哪裡?

Can you give me the direction to xx?
你能給我 xx 的方向嗎?

What direction should I follow?
我應該往哪個方向?

How can I get to xx?
xx 怎麼走?

I don't know where I am.
我不知道這裡是什麼地方。

What street am I on?
我在哪一條街上?

Where am I on this map?
我在地圖上的什麼地方?

無法回答他人問路時

I am a stranger here. (080)
我第一次來。

I am also new here.
我也是第一次來。

I don't know, sorry.
抱歉，我不清楚

You're right here
你在這兒

First-Aid
Vocabulary

生理衛生

● 情緒表達

笑，哭

smile	微笑	(081)
smirk	假笑	
snicker	竊笑 嘻嘻作笑	
chuckle	輕笑	
giggle	傻笑	
grin	嬉笑	
guffaw	狂笑 捧腹大笑	
laugh	大笑	
cackle	尖笑	
gloat	得意 幸災樂禍	
cry	哭泣	
moan	嗚咽	
weep	哭泣	

驚愕，冷靜

amaze	驚愕
shocked	震驚
surprised	驚訝
cold	冷酷
calm	平靜
ponder	沉思

憤怒，煩躁

angry	憤怒	082
glare	怒視	
roar	怒吼	
snarl	怒罵	
snub	斥責	
frown	皺眉	
fidget	煩躁，動來動去 坐立不安	
indignant	憤怒的	
mad	發狂的 瘋狂的	
outrageous	勃然大怒的	
irritating	氣人的	
furious	狂怒的	
quarrelsome	愛爭吵的	
bad-tempered	脾氣不好的	

害羞，好奇，迷惑

bashful	害羞
shy	害羞
curious	好奇
confuse	迷惑

驚慌，可怕，遲疑

horrible	可怕的
dreadful	可怕的
cower	膽怯

cowardly	膽怯的
cringe	畏縮
panic	恐慌
horrify	使恐懼
frighten	驚恐 使驚恐
boggle hesitate	猶豫

疲倦，無聊，哀傷，痛苦

yawn	呵欠
tired	疲倦
bored	無聊
sigh	歎息
groan	呻吟
whine	牢騷
mourn	哀悼
regretful	後悔的

惡意的

hostile	敵意的 不友好的
spiteful	懷恨的 惡意的
snobbish	勢利的
malicious	懷惡意的 惡毒的
wicked	邪惡的

mischievous	調皮的 (083)
	惡意的
vicious	惡意的

憂鬱，低落，煩惱，悲傷，失望

moody	憂鬱的，易怒的
sullen	抑鬱的，沈悶的
melancholy	憂鬱的
anxious	發愁的，不安的
despair	絕望
disappointed	失望的
frustrated	沮喪的
gloomy	抑鬱的，悲觀的
grief	悲痛
upset	傷心的
sorrowful	悲傷的
troubled	煩惱的
down-hearted	情緒低落的

● 形容個性常用詞

聰明	
alert	機敏的
	警覺的
witty	機智的
	愛說風趣話的

shrewd	精明的 機敏的
sharp-minded	機智的
intelligent smart	聰明的
watchful	機敏的
sensible	明智的
ingenious	心靈手巧的
talent	天才 有才能的人

愚笨	
ignorant	無知的
clumsy	笨拙的
stupid silly	愚笨的
awkward	尷尬的，笨拙的

好奇，有創意	
creative	有創意的
curious	好奇的

仁慈，寬容，溫和，同情	
charitable	慈善的 慷慨的
benevolent humane merciful	仁慈的，人道的， 寬大的

tolerant	容忍的 寬容的	(084)
compassion	同情	
compassionate sympathetic	有同情心的	
mild	温和的	

謙恭，有理，體貼，有耐心

humble	謙恭的
courteous	有禮貌的
thoughtful	體貼的
patient	有耐心的

熱情，熱心，鼓舞

sociable	愛交際的
hospitable	殷勤好客的
hearty cordial	衷心的，熱誠的， 友善的
warmhearted enthusiastic	熱心的
inspirational	鼓舞人心的

安靜，拘謹，順從，謹慎

silent	安靜的
self-controlled	鎮靜的
reserved restrained	拘謹的，有克制的 有節制的
obedient	聽話的 順從的

careful	小心的
cautious	謹慎的
conservative	保守的

虛偽，不誠實

insincere	不真誠的
dishonest	不誠實的
deceitful	欺詐的，不老實的
hypocritical	虛偽的

真誠，大方，可信賴，有擔當

frank	坦白的，直率的
genuine	真誠的，坦率的
generous	大方的，慷慨的
earnest	認真的，誠摯的
straightforward	正直，老實，簡單
sincere	認真的 真心的
reliable	可依賴的
trustworthy	可信任的
dependable	可信賴的

輕蔑，膚淺，驕傲

scornful	輕蔑的 蔑視的
superficial shallow	膚淺的
showy	炫耀的
pretentious	矯飾的

extravagant	奢侈的	(085)
conceited	驕傲的	
	自負的	

粗心大意，不認真，疏忽

ill-advised	輕率的，不明智的
unintentional	無意的
uninformed	無知的
	不學無術的
impulsive	衝動的，莽撞的
rude	魯莽的
hasty	倉促的，草率的
careless	粗心大意的
thoughtless	
half-hearted	不認真的
neglectful	疏忽的
offensive	討厭的，無禮的
reckless	不計後果的
impatient	不耐煩的

公正無私，正派的

impartial	公正的
disinterested	
unselfish	無私的
detached	不偏不倚的
	超然的
decent	正派的，像樣的

快樂，天真，無憂無慮，幽默的

cheerful	歡樂的
carefree	無憂無慮的
ingenuous	天真無邪的
naive	天真的 幼稚的
optimistic	樂觀的
humorous	幽默的

有能力，有效率，無能力

competent	有才能的
incompetent	不勝任的
capable	有能力的
incapable	無能的
effective	有效的
efficient	效率高的
productive	有成效的
versatile	多才多藝的
irresponsible	不負責任的

冷漠，不關心，勉強

merciless	冷酷無情的
indifferent	漠不關心的
unconcerned	不關心的
reluctant	不願意的

節儉，勤奮，吝嗇

frugal	勤儉節約的 (086)
economical **thrifty**	節儉的，節約的
diligent **laborious**	勤奮的
stingy	吝嗇的

多愁善感，憂鬱，軟弱

sentimental	多愁善感的
passionate	易動情的
inactive	無生氣的 不快活的
depressed	壓抑的
pessimistic	悲觀的
uneasy	焦慮不安的
dependent	依賴的
fragile	脆弱的 易碎的

叛逆，挑戰，野心勃勃的

disobedient	不順從的
challenging	挑戰的
dominant	支配的，統治的
interfere	干涉，干預
intrusive	闖入的

堅定，頑固，古怪

persevering	持之以恆的
persistent	堅持不懈的
insistent	堅持的
obstinate	頑固的，固執的
eccentric **odd** **strange**	古怪的，奇怪的

其他

daring **bold**	大膽的
unpunctual	不準時的
narrow-minded	心胸狹窄的
suspicious	多疑的
bias	偏心
character **disposition**	性格
characteristic	特性，特徵
temperament	氣質，稟性

● 身體動作

眼耳鼻口動作

peer	偷窺	(087)
gaze	凝視	
blink	眨眼	
stare	盯視	
nod	點頭	
see	看見	
read	讀書	
listen	聆聽	
smell	聞	
breathe	呼吸	
shout	呼喊	
burp	打嗝	
sniff	吸氣	
sneeze	打噴嚏	
whistle	口哨	
shoo	驅趕 用"噓"聲趕走	
cheer	歡呼	
praise	讚美	
cough	咳嗽	
drink	喝酒	
eat	進食	
gasp	喘氣	
lick	舔舌	
talk	談話	

taunt	嘲弄
applaud	喝彩
sing	唱歌
spit	吐出
bite	啃咬
whisper	耳語 低聲說出
murmur	喃喃自語
plead	懇求
scream	尖叫
speak	說話
blow	吹

腿部動作

beg	跪求
kneel	跪拜，跪著
kick	踢
stand	站立
grovel	曲膝匍匐
bounce	蹦跳
jump	跳
climb	爬
crawl	爬行
walk	走路
run	跑
ride	騎
curtsy	行禮 女子行屈膝禮

軀幹動作

bow	鞠躬	(088)
shiver	打顫	
shake	顫抖	
shimmy	擺動	
apology	道歉	
sit	坐下	
sleep	睡覺	
lay down	躺下	
hug	緊擁	
cuddle	擁抱	
duck	閃避	
dance	跳舞	
fart	放屁	
tease	挑逗	
shrug	聳肩	

手部動作

raise	舉手
crack	響指
dig	挖
cut	切
nose pick	挖鼻子
tap	輕拍
poke	手戳
salute	敬禮
hail	致敬

shoot	射擊
wave	揮手
clap	鼓掌
surrender	投降
slap	摑…耳光
bye	再見
tickle	撓癢
scratch	抓癢
welcome	歡迎
beckon	招手
greet	問候
kiss	飛吻
point	指點
massage	按摩
open	打開
write	寫
carry	提
pull	拉
push	推
hit	打
	打擊
throw	丟
touch	摸
	接觸
wash	洗
wipe	擦拭
sew	縫

knit	編織	(089)
draw	劃(線)	
paint	繪畫	
brush	刷	
knock	敲	
bring	攜帶	
drive	開車	
fix	修理	

其他動作

thank	感謝
threaten	恐嚇
rude	粗魯
insult	侮辱
comfort	安慰
bush	埋伏
ready	就緒
play	遊戲
congratulate	恭喜
wait	等待
stop	停止
sweep	清掃
think	想
sleep	睡覺
wake	清醒
move	移動
fantastic	太好了
forgive	原諒

● 成長發育

成長發育常用字

growth	生長
development	發育
maturity	成熟
physical development	身體發育
sexual prematurely	性早熟
masturbation	手淫
spermatorrhea	夢遺
menarche age	月經初潮年齡
delayed puberty	性發育延遲
contraceptive	避孕藥
birth control	避孕
secondary sex characters	第二性徵
nutrition	營養
malnutrition	營養不良
endocrine	內分泌
insufficiency	不足
intake	攝取

人生各時期

fetal stage	胎兒期
ovi-germ stage	胚卵期
embryo stage	胚胎期

neonatal period	新生兒期 (090)
term infant	足月兒
premature	早產兒
post term infant	過期產兒
perinatal stage	圍產期 出生前後時期
infancy	嬰兒期
baby	嬰兒
little baby	幼嬰
infant	嬰兒
childhood	童年期
toddler age	幼兒期
preschool age	學齡前
school age	學齡期
kid	兒童
child	兒童
little child	幼童
prepuberty	青春早期
puberty	發育期，青春期
adolescence	青春期 **puberty** 至 **adulthood** 之間的 過程。
prepubescence	青春前期
postpubescence	青春後期
boy	男孩
little boy	小男孩

girl	女孩
little girl	小女孩
youngster	小孩，年輕人
young man	小夥子
youth	青少年
teenager	青春期的孩子
juvenile	
adolescent	
maturity	成人期
adulthood	
adult	成人
grown-up	成人的
man	男人
men	男人(複數)
woman	女人
women	女人(複數)
manhood	男性成年期
womanhood	女性成年期
menopause	更年期
old age	老年期
old	老的
aged	老
elderly	上了年紀的
in years	老年

● 身體構造

骨骼

bone	骨	(091)
skeleton	骨骼	
spinal marrow	脊髓	
spine vertebra backbone	脊椎	
skull	顱骨 頭蓋骨	
cheek bone	顴骨	
collarbone	鎖骨	
rib	肋骨	
breastbone	胸骨	
joint	關節	
pelvis	骨盆	

肌肉

muscle	肌肉
sinew	腱

血管

blood vessel	血管
vein	靜脈
artery	動脈
capillary	毛細血管

口腔

tongue	舌頭
oral cavity	口腔
oral epithelium	口腔上皮
epithelium	上皮
mouth floor	口底
saliva	唾液(口水)
dribble **drool**	流口水
palate	顎
masticatory muscle	咬合肌肉
taste bud	味蕾

牙齒

tooth	牙齒
denture	假齒
dental crown	牙冠
gum	牙齦
incisor	門齒
molar	臼齒 大牙
wisdom tooth	智齒
milk tooth	乳齒
deciduous teeth	乳牙
permanent teeth	恆牙

頭部

head	頭	(092)
brain	腦	
hair	頭髮	
left hemisphere	左腦	
right hemisphere	右腦	

臉部

skin	皮膚
wrinkle	皺紋
face	臉
forehead	額頭
eye brow	眉毛
eye	眼
lid	眼瞼
nose	鼻子
nose ridge	鼻梁
nostril	鼻孔
temple	太陽穴
cheek	臉頰
dimple	酒窩
mouth	嘴
lip	嘴唇
chin	下巴
sideburns	鬢角
ear	耳

肩頸部

neck	脖子
throat	咽喉
tonsil	扁桃腺
windpipe	氣管
bronchus	支氣管
shoulder	肩

胸部

diaphragm	隔膜
chest	胸部
gullet esophagus	食道
heart	心臟
atrium	心房
ventricle	心室
lung	肺
breast	乳房
nipple papilla tit	乳頭
areola	乳暈

背臀部

back	背
hip	臀部
breech	臀

buttock bottom	屁股	(093)
anus	肛門	

腰腹部

navel belly button	肚臍
abdomen	腹部
waist	腰
gall	膽汁
gall bladder	膽囊
kidney	腎臟
liver	肝臟
pancreas	胰腺
spleen	脾
stomach	胃
bladder	膀胱
small intestine	小腸
large intestine	大腸
duodenum	十二指腸
appendix	盲腸
rectum	直腸

男女性徵

penis	陰莖
testicle testis	睪丸
balls	陰囊(口語)

peanut	男性生殖器官(口語)
scrotum	陰囊
urine	尿道
ovary	卵巢
uterus **womb**	子宮
vagina	陰道
pubic hair	陰毛
armpit hair	腋毛

腳

foot	腳
instep	腳背
toe	腳趾
ankle	踝
heel	腳後跟
sole	腳底
arch	腳掌心
thigh	大腿
kneecap	膝蓋骨
knee	膝蓋
shank	小腿
calf	小腿肚

手

thumb	大拇指
forefinger **index finger**	食指

		094
middle finger	中指	
ring finger	無名指	
little finger **pinkie**	小指	
palm	手掌 手心	
nail	指甲	
fist	拳頭	
knuckle	指關節	
back of the hand	手背	
wrist	手腕	
elbow	肘	
armpit	腋下	

其他

extremities	四肢 手足
trunk	軀幹
organ	器官
nerve	神經
lymph	淋巴腺
circulatory system	循環系統

● 檢查治療

醫學檢查常見詞彙

prescription	處方
diagnose	診斷
clinic	診所
symptom	症狀
treatment	治療
examination	檢查
general check-up physical examination	健康診斷
ECG, electrocardiogram	心電圖
mammography	乳房攝影
vaginal laparoscope	陰道鏡
cervical smear	子宮頸抹片
smear	抹片
biopsy	切片檢查
national health insurance	全民健保
prevention	預防
build	體格
blood	血液
blood type	血型
tuberculin reaction	結核反應
congenital	先天性病
relative	親戚
heredity	遺傳
immunity	免疫

diagnosis	診斷	(095)
quarantine	檢疫 隔離	
suspected	疑似	
affect	感染	
infection		
epidemic	流行性的	
incubation	潛伏期	
virus	濾過性病毒	
disorder	失調	
chronic	慢性的	
acute	急症 急性的	
pulse rate	脈搏數	
pulsation		
rapid pulse	快脈	
irregular pulse	不規則脈	
respiration rate	呼吸數	
breath	呼吸	
respiration		
death rate	死亡率	
crude cancer incidence rate	癌症粗發生率	
chronic disease	慢性疾病	
red cell	紅血球	
white cell	白血球	
bowel movement	排便	

blood analysis **blood test**	驗血
Celsius, centigrade	攝氏
Fahrenheit	華式
thermometer	體溫計
stool	便
loose stool	軟便
bloody stool	血便
mucous stool	粘液便
clay-colored stool	粘土便
urine	尿
bloody urine	血尿
cloudy urine	尿混濁
pyuria	膿尿
glycosuria	糖尿
relapse	復發症
casualty	急症
serous	血清的
confirmed	確認的
offensive	刺激性的
admission to hospital	入院
discharge from hospital	退院
clinical history	病歷
blood pressure	血壓

● 檢查治療

醫學治療詞彙

resection	切除	(096)
prescription	藥方	
operation	手術	
irrigation	沖洗	
enema	灌腸	
serum	血清	
anesthesia	麻醉	
local anesthesia	局部麻醉	
general anesthesia	麻醉全身	
intravenous anesthesia	靜脈麻醉	
spinal anesthesia	脊椎麻醉	
vaccinate	注射疫苗 種牛痘	
injection	打針 注射	
I.V., intravenous drip	點滴	
aromatherapy	芳香治療法	
massage	推拿	
chiropractic	整脊	
side effect	副作用	
ultrared ray infrared ray	紅外線	
UV; ultraviolet ray	紫外線	

藥品名稱

pain killer	止痛藥(針)
aspirin	阿斯匹靈
ointment	軟膏
eye medicine	眼藥
medicine **drug**	藥
tablet **pill**	藥丸
capsule	膠囊
cough medicine	止咳藥
sublingual tablet	舌下錠
suppository	栓劑
antibiotic	抗生素
medicine	藥品
enema	灌腸劑
drug	藥
toxic	有毒
toxicant	毒品
heroin	海洛因
morphine	嗎啡
quietive	鎮靜劑

● 疾病症狀

四肢及骨骼

stiffness in shoulder	肩膀僵硬	(097)
back pain	背痛	
scoliosis	脊椎側彎 脊柱側凸	
lordosis	脊椎側彎 脊柱前凸	
kyphosis	脊椎側彎 脊柱後凸 駝背	
low back pain	腰痛	
sprain	扭傷	
graze	擦傷 抓破	
dislocation	脫臼	
fracture	骨折	
cramp	抽筋 痙攣	
bruise	淤傷 淤青	
trauma	外傷	
scratch	擦傷 抓傷	
scrap	擦傷	
twist	扭傷	
cut	割傷	
handicapped	殘廢	

胸腔

chest pain	胸痛
pneumonia	肺炎
heart disease	心臟病
heart attach	心臟病發作
myocardial infraction	心肌梗塞
heart failure	心臟衰弱
congenital heart disease	
	先天性心臟疾病
arteriosclerosis	動脈硬化症
angina	狹心症
cardiac neurosis	心臟神經症
cardiac asthma	心臟喘息
myocarditis	心肌炎
endocarditic	心內膜炎
valvular cyanosis	心臟瓣膜疾病
arrhythmia	心律不整
pleurisy	胸膜炎
bronchitis	支氣管炎
bronchial asthma	支氣管氣喘
pulmonary	肺氣腫
respiratory system	呼吸系統
difficult in breathing	呼吸困難
expiration	呼氣
inspiration	吸氣
bradycardia	心搏徐緩
short of breath	不能呼吸

頭部及耳鼻喉

fever	發燒	(098)
high fever	高燒	
headache	頭痛	
migraine	偏頭痛	
earache	耳痛	
deaf	聾	
sore throat	喉嚨痛	
stuffy nose	鼻塞	
running nose	流鼻涕	
wheezing	哮喘	
tinnitus	耳鳴	
sneeze	打噴嚏	
cough	咳嗽	
dry cough	乾咳	
moist cough	有痰咳	
hemoptysis	咳血	
blood-spitting	吐血	
pharyngitis	咽頭炎	
huskiness	聲音沙啞	
hoarseness	沙啞	
sputum	痰	
snore	打鼾	
hiccup	打嗝	

眼睛

astigmatism	散光
myopia nearsightedness	近視
hyperopia farsightedness	遠視
color blindness	色盲
trachoma	沙眼
cataract	白內障
blind	盲
sty	針眼
conjunctivitis	結膜炎
eyelash poke into the eyes	
	睫毛倒插

口腔疾病

gingivitis	牙齦炎
toothache	牙齒痛
periodontosis	牙周病
plaque	牙菌斑
fill	補牙
decay	蛀牙
cavity caries	齲齒
bad breath	口臭
lip crack	嘴唇乾裂

傳染病

acute infectious diseases	急性傳染病 (099)
flu, influenza	流感
infectious diseases	傳染病
cold	感冒
	傷風
	著涼
dysentery	痢疾
tetanus	破傷風
cholera	霍亂
malaria	瘧疾
scarlet fever	猩紅熱
mumps	流行性腮腺炎
syphilis	梅毒
tetanus	破傷風
rabies	狂犬病
bronchitis	支氣管炎
diphtheria	白喉
pneumonia	肺炎
typhus	斑疹傷寒
measles	麻疹
T.B., tuberculosis	肺結核
phthisis	肺結核
	癆病
pulmonary tuberculosis	
chicken pox	水痘

腹腔疾病（肝膽腸胃脾腎）

abdominal pain	腹痛
abdominal enlargement	腹部膨脹
digestive system	消化系統
appendicitis	盲腸炎
stomachache	胃痛或引申為腹痛
gastritis	胃炎
gastritis ulcer	胃潰瘍
nephritis	腎炎
hyperacidity	胃酸過多症
indigestion	消化不良
diarrhea	腹瀉
loose stool	軟便
bloody stool	血便
mucous stool	粘液便
bloody urine	血尿
cloudy urine	尿混濁
pyuria	膿尿
constipation	便秘
hepatitis	肝炎
cirrhosis of the liver	肝硬化
appendicitis	闌尾炎
peritonitis	腹膜炎
intestinal tuberculosis	腸結核
rumbling sound	腸鳴
intestinal catarrh	腸黏膜炎

colitis	大腸炎	(100)
duodenal ulcer	十二指腸潰瘍	
volvulus	腸扭結	
cholecystitis	膽炎	
gall stone	膽結石症	
jaundice	黃疸	
pancreatitis	胰臟炎	
pass gas fart	放屁	
anorexia	食慾不振	
intussusception	腸套腸	
ascariasis	蛔蟲病	

心理疾病

neurasthenia	神經衰弱
epilepsy	癲癇
insanity	精神病
insomnia	失眠症

女性相關

anemia	貧血
pregnancy conceive	懷孕
labor pain	分娩陣痛
period	月經
menstrual pain	經痛
miscarriage abortion	流產

腫瘤

cancer	癌
tumor	腫瘤
in situ carcinoma	原位癌
invasive cancer	侵襲癌
nasopharyngeal carcinoma	鼻咽癌
thyroid cancer	甲狀腺癌
cancer of the oral cavity	口腔癌
skin cancer	皮膚癌
leukemla	白血病
rectal cancer	直腸癌
cancer of the colon and rectum	結直腸癌
esophagus cancer	食道癌
stomach cancer gastric cancer	胃癌
intestine cancer	小腸癌
liver cancer	肝癌
lung cancer	肺癌
bladder cancer	膀胱癌
breast cancer	乳癌
cancer of the womb	子宮體癌
cervical cancer	子宮頸癌
prostate cancer	攝護腺癌
radiation pain	放射痛

皮膚

skin disease	皮膚病	(101)
sunburn	太陽晒傷	
burn	燙傷	
	燒傷	
acne	痘痘	
freckle	雀斑	
pimple	面皰	
	暗瘡	
mole	痣	
birthmark	胎記	
nevus	痣	
dermatitis	皮膚炎	
contact dermatitis	接觸性皮膚炎	
scaly skin	麟狀皮	
eczema	濕疹	
infantile eczema	小兒濕疹	
seborrhea eczema	脂漏性濕疹	
measles	麻疹	
urticaria	蕁麻疹	
	風疹塊	
drug eruption	藥疹	
rash	疹	
red rash	紅疹	
roseola	玫瑰疹	

tinea	癬
psoriasis	牛皮癬
scabies	疥
frost bite	凍瘡
scalding	燙傷
lupus	狼瘡
corn	雞眼
athletes foot	香港腳
wart	疣
boil	瘡
gangrene	壞疽

皮膚的感覺

itch	癢
itchy	癢癢的
itching	發癢
tingling	刺刺的
pain	痛
painful	痛痛的
hurt	痛
touch	觸覺
burn	灼傷
dry	(傷口周圍)乾乾的

外傷處理

wound	傷口	(102)
unintentional injury	意外傷害	
external wound	外傷	
wound management	傷口護理	
wound margin	傷口周邊	
wound depth	傷口深度	
sterilization	消毒	
infection	感染	
discolored	(指皮膚) 變色的	
color	(傷口)顏色	
swell	(傷口)腫脹	
edema	(傷口)水腫	
exudate	滲出物 組織液	
tissue	組織	
brown necrotic tissue	棕色壞死組	
slough	腐肉	
granulation	肉芽(形成)	
blood stain	血污	
purulent	化膿的	
bleeding	流血的 出血的	
bleeding badly	留了很多血	
the volume of bleeding	出血量	
odor	味道(異味)	
inflamed	發炎的	

形容痛覺

ache, pain	痛
no pain not pain	不會痛
mild pain slight pain moderate pain	一點點痛 輕微的痛
severe pain acute pain	很痛，嚴重疼痛
intermittent pain pain come at intervals	一陣一陣的痛
constant pain continuous pain persistent pain	持續的痛
(feel pain) at dressing change	換藥時才會痛
tingling pain prickling pain piercing pain	刺痛
throbbing pain	抽痛
sharp pain	急劇的痛，刺痛
dull pain	鈍痛，暗痛
pressing pain	按壓時會痛
burning pain	灼痛
tearing pain	撕裂般疼痛
sore pain	腫痛
crushing pain	壓迫痛
ache all over	全身疼痛

colic	絞痛 🎧103
	尤指腹痛
cramping pain	絞痛
crampy pain	痙攣痛
distended pain	脹痛
radiating pain	擴散痛
stabbing pain	刀刺痛
sore pain	潰爛痛

其他症狀

hay fever	花粉症
disease	疾病
uncomfortable	不舒服
body odor	狐臭
	體臭
heat stroke	中暑
poisoning	中毒
endemic	水土不服
stupor	昏迷
coma	昏迷狀態
shock	休克
allergy	過敏
faint	暈倒
difficulty in swallowing	吞嚥困難
inflammation	發炎

ulcer	潰瘍
neuralgia	神經痛
paralysis	麻痺
poliomyelitis	脊髓灰質炎
diabetes	糖尿病
rheumatism	風濕病
arthritis	關節炎
stroke	中風
hemiplegia	半身不遂
septicemia	敗血病
hypertension	高血壓
hypotension	低血壓
anemic	貧血的
palpitation	心悸
thrombosis	血栓症
aneurysm	動脈瘤
anus fistula	瘺管 痔瘺
hemorrhoids piles	痔瘡
sense of pressure	壓迫感
hunger pain	飢餓痛
nausea	噁心
vomit	嘔吐
shuddering	發抖

		🎧 104
chill	打冷顫 畏寒	
night sweat	盜汗	
sweat	發汗	
pale **pallor**	臉色發白	
asthenia	虛弱	
fatigue	疲勞	
cyanosis	發紺， 皮膚呈青紫色	
tiredness	倦怠	
obesity	肥胖症	
heat exhaustion	輕度中暑 熱衰竭	
heat stroke	中暑	
asthma	哮喘	
electric shock	觸電	
injury	受傷	
bleeding	出血	

First-Aid Vocabulary

Chapter

6

商用英語

商用英語
業務英語
價格談判
辦公室英語
辦公室設備
書信及電話
會議英語
評論數據

● 商用英語

貿易常用詞彙

trade	貿易	(105)
trading	貿易的 交易的	
commerce	商業 貿易 交易	
internal trade **inland trade** **domestic trade**	國內貿易	
international trade	國際貿易	
foreign trade **external trade**	外貿	
triangle sales **triangular sales**	三角貿易	

進出口

import **importation**	進口，輸入
export **exportation**	出口
transit trade	轉口貿易
tax rebate	出口退稅

貿易政策

bonded warehouse	保稅倉庫	(106)
free-trade area	自由貿易區	
special preferences	優惠關稅	
tariff barrier	關稅壁壘	
favorable balance of trade		
	貿易順差	
unfavorable balance of trade		
	貿易逆差	

貿易商

wholesaler	批發商
manufacturer	製造商 製造廠
dealer distributor	經銷商
retailer tradesman	零售商
retail trade	零售業
merchant	商人
competitor	競爭者 對手 敵手
middleman agent	中間商 經紀人 掮客
importer	進口商
exporter	出口商

貿易夥伴

trade partner	貿易伙伴
buyer	買方
seller	賣方
consumer	消費者 用戶
consumption	消費
client customer	顧客，客戶

銷售管道

channel	途徑 管道 手段
commercial channel	商業管道
distribution channel	銷售管道
bulk sale	整批銷售
wholesale	批發
outlet	銷路 商店 商行
monopoly	壟斷
market	市場
home market	國內市場
open market	公開市場
black market	黑市

業績管理

commission	佣金 107
sales figure	業績數字
revenue turnover volume of business	營業額，銷售額

預算及訂單流程

foresight forecast budget	預測，預算
goods	商品
offer	報價
inquiry	詢價
order	訂單
sale	銷售

交貨流程

delivery make delivery	交貨
make prompt delivery	馬上交貨
partial delivery partial shipment	分批交貨
ship	裝運，出貨
shipment	裝載的貨物

付款流程

payment	支付 付款
pay	付款 支付 償還
deferred payment	延期付款
expedite payment	催款

採購及存貨流程

purchase	採購 進貨
demand	需求
supply	供應
inventory	存貨
stock	庫存 庫存量

品管流程

quality	品質
QC; Quality Control	品質管制
QA; Quality Assurance	品管
quality control circle	品管圖
IPQC; Inprocess Quality Control	製成品管
FQC; Finish Quality Control	成品品管
OQC; Outgoing Quality Control	出貨品管

貿易常用英文縮寫

DOC: document	文件 單據	(108)
C.O.: certificate of origin	一般原產地證	
C/D: customs declaration	報關單	
P/L: packing list	裝箱單 明細表	
INV: invoice	發票	
S/C: sales contract	銷售確認書	
B/L: bill of lading	提單	
T, LTX, TX;telex	電傳	
EMS; express mail special	特快郵遞	
W; with	具有	
w/o; without	沒有	
G.S.P.; generalized system of preferences	普惠制	
DL, DLS; dollar/dollars	美元	
RMB; renminbi	人民幣	
M/V; merchant vessel	商船	
S.S; steamship	船運	
WT; weight	重量	
G.W.; gross weight	毛重	
N.W.; net weight	淨重	
PCT; percent	百分比	

FAC; facsimile	傳真
IMP; import	進口
EXP; export	出口
MT, M/T; metric ton	公噸
MAX; maximum	最大的 最大限度的
MIN; minimum	最小的 最低限度
M, MED; medium	中等 中級的
INT; international	國際的
STL.; style	式樣 款式 類型
PUR; purchase	購買 購貨
S/M; shipping marks	裝船標記
REF; reference	參考 查價
PR, PRC; price	價格
EA; each	每個，各
CTN, CTNS; carton/cartons	紙箱
PC, PCE, PCS piece/pieces	只，個，支等
DOZ, DZ; dozen	一打
PKG; package	一包 一捆 一件等

● 業務英語

行銷英語

catalogue	目錄
logo	商標
flyer leaflet DM promotional flyer brochure	傳單 單張印刷品 文宣品
brochure stand brochure holder	文宣展示架
booklet brochure handbook pamphlet manual	小冊子
poster	海報
flag	布條 旗幟
flag pole	旗竿
advertise	為…做廣告 為…宣傳
sample	樣本
gift	贈品
promote	宣傳，推銷 (商品等)
opportunity	機會
marketing	行銷

業務拜訪

business card **card**	名片
pay visit	拜訪
representative	代表
sales representative	銷售代表 業務員
approach	接觸
invite	邀請
meet with (+sb)	與 (某人) 見面
appointment	約會
shake hands	握手
postpone	延期
make an appointment	預約 約見
reschedule	改期
notify	通知
cancel	取消

退換貨要求

return	退貨
replace	換貨
exchange	交換
defect goods	品質不良的產品
lodge a claim (+with/against)	提出(申訴，抗議等)
file a claim (+with/against)	提出(申訴，抗議等)

商品品質

quality	品質
quality control	品質管理
quality certificate	品質證明書
qualify	證明...合格
unsatisfactory	不滿意的
satisfactory	令人滿意的 符合要求的 良好的
good quality	好品質
fine quality	優質
best quality	最好的品質
choice quality selected quality	精選的品質
prime quality tip-top quality	第一流的品質
first-rate quality first-class quality	頭等的品質
high quality	高品質
better quality superior in quality	較好的品質
sound quality	完好的品質
fair quality	尚好的品質
average quality	平均品質
common quality	一般品質
standard quality	標準品質

usual quality	通常的品質
popular quality	大眾化的品質
uniform quality	一律的品質
inferior quality	較次的品質
be inferior to	次於…
bad quality	劣質
poor quality	品質較差
low quality	低品質

below the average quality
一般水平以下的品質

above the average quality
一般水準以上的品質

索賠

compensate	賠償 補償
claim	索賠
make a claim register a claim raise a claim put in a claim bring up a claim	提出索賠
make a claim with sb. make a claim against sb.	向某方提出索賠
make a claim for sth. make a claim on sth.	就某事提出索賠

管理詞彙

administration	管理
management	
organization	組織
authorize	授權給…
potential market	潛在市場 市場潛力
marketing	銷售學 銷售業務 市場調查
cost of production	生產成本
long standing relationship	
long term relationship	長久貿易關係
transaction	交易
plan	計劃
planning	計劃編制
program	計劃 方案
survey	調查 問卷調查
expanding market	擴大銷路 成長中的市場
be equivalent to	相當於
utmost	竭盡所能

商用報表

outline	提綱，概要 要點，草案
summary	總結 摘要 一覽
recap **recapitulation**	重述要點
consolidate	彙總
by date	逐日的
by week	逐週的
by month	逐月的
by quarter	逐季的
stress	著重
highlight	使顯著 使突出 強調
figure	數字 數據
ratio	比例
rate	比例 率 比率 費用 價格

● 價格談判

詢價

enquiry, inquiry	詢價	(112)
inquirer	詢價者	
specific inquiry	具體詢價	
an occasional inquiry	偶而詢價	
heavy enquiries	大量詢價	
RFQ; request for quotation		
make an enquiry		
enquiry about	發出詢價	
reply an enquiry	回覆詢價	
receive an enquiry	接到詢價	

報價

quote	報價
quotation	
offer	
make an offer	
official offer	正式報價
special offer	特別優惠
offer for	報價 提供
forward an offer send an offer	送出報價
give an offer	給報價
submit an offer	提出報價
preferential offer	(關稅)優惠的報價
lump offer 綜合報價(針對兩種以上商品)	

接受報價

get an offer	拿到報價
obtain an offer	獲得報價
accept an offer	接受報價
use	採用，結算
adopt	(幣值或價格條件)
employ	結算
	用...計價
	採用...幣值
meet (the price/enquiry)	滿足 (價格 / 需求)

還價

decline the offer	拒絕此報價
turn down the offer	
withdraw	取消
	撤回
	撤銷
counter offer	還價
reply an offer	答覆報價
say 5% lower	譬如說減 5%
make it $$$$!	算你$$$$ (金額)!
entertain an offer	考慮報價
bargain	討價還價

競標

bid	出價，喊價，投標
make a bid	競標
get a bid	得到競標

outbid	在競標中得標 🎧113
auction	拍賣,競標

價格有效期限

the offer is for 3 days	
	此報價 3 天內有效
valid	有效(期限)
expire	滿期,屆期, (期限) 終止
extend the offer	延長報價有效期限
offering period	報價有效期限
renew an offer reinstate an offer	延長報價有效期限

定價類別

price	價格
price per unit	單價
per	每(單位)
buying price	買價
selling price	賣價
pricing method	定價方法
price tag	價格標籤

價格表

rate	費率
price list	價目表
price format	價格表
priced	已標價的 有定價的

pricing	定價
	標價
price of factory	廠價
price card	價格目錄

影響價格的條件

international market price	
world market price	國際市場價格
price index	物價指數
price indices	
price effect	價格效應
price limit	價格限制
price control	價格控制
price theory	價格理論
price regulation	價格調整
price support	價格支援
sales condition	銷售條件
exchange rate fluctuation	
	匯率浮動

價格談判

lowest possible price	可能最低價
highest possible price	可能最高價
wild speculation	漫天要價
price is stiff	價格堅挺的
	昂貴的
prohibitive	(價格)過高的
reasonable	合理

profit	利潤	(114)
price is easy	價格疲軟	
cut price	削價	
lower (the price)	降低(價格)	
go lower	降低一點	
reduce (the price)	減價	

參考價格

indicative price	參考價格
nominal price	名義上的價格
	非市場價值
average price	平均價格
market price	市價

估價、待確認價格

non-firm offer	未確認的報價
estimate	估計，預估，估價
estimation	
valuation	

原價、現行價格

firm price	實價
firm offer	
original price	原價
maintain original price	
	維持原價

current price	時價
present price	
current price	
prevailing price	
ruling price	
going price	

最高、最低、成本價

ceiling price	最高價
maximum price	
minimum price	最低價
rock-bottom price	
bedrock price	
base price	底價
cost price	成本價

優惠價格

discount	折扣
price is favorable	價格優惠
favorable	優惠的
exceptional price	特價
special price	

價格策略

term	條件
payment term	付款方式
payment	付款
cash sale	現金交易
currency	貨幣

credit	信用	〔115〕
allot	分配 (數量)	
freight	運費	
cost	成本	
pricing policy	價格策略	
price contract	價格合約	
price calculation	價格計算	
extra price	附加價	
exchange rate	匯率	
price structure	價格構成	
pass over	轉給 轉嫁	
trade term price term	價格條件	
spot price	現貨價格	
commission	佣金	
discount allowance	折扣	

其他	
moderate price	公平價格
best price	最好的價格
new price	新價
old price	舊價
opening price	開價 開盤價
closing price	收盤價
wholesale price	批發價

retail price	零售價
net price	淨價
gross price	毛價

● 辦公室英語

人事規定

ID card	識別證
lunch hour	中午休息時間
office hours	辦公時間
turnover	人員更替率 營業額 交易額 證券成交額
lay off	解僱
promotion	升職
performance evaluation	
	考績評核
evaluation sheet	考績評鑑卡
incentive system	激勵制度
incentive wage	激勵獎金
incentive tour	獎勵旅遊
raise	加薪
salary	薪水

工作夥伴

fellow	夥伴，同事
coworker	一同工作的人 同事

employee	雇員	116
	員工	
employer	雇主	
staff	員工	

職務代理

acting	代理的
acting manager	代理經理
deputy	代理人
p.p.; per pro	代簽
job replacement	接替工作(的人)
job successor	繼承工作(的人)
job substitution	代理工作(的人)
	代班者
authorize	授權給
	委託
assign	指派
	指定
authorization	授權
	認可
authority	職權
	當權者
	當局
in charge of	管理，照料
handle	
take care of	照顧

上下班，輪班，休假

closed	本日公休
clock in punch in	打卡上班
clock out punch out	打卡下班
at work	在上班
on duty	在勤
off duty	下班
work double shifts	輪值兩班
work two jobs	兼兩份工作
day shift regular shift	日班
night shift	晚班(小夜班)
graveyard shift	夜班(大夜班)
on leave absence day-off	請假
annual leave	年假
business leave	公假
military leave	兵役假
sick leave	病假
personal leave compassionate leave	事假
wedding leave	婚假

maternity leave	產假	(117)
menstruation leave	生理假	
compensation off compensatory leave deferred leave	補休	

辦公室職稱

Chairman	總裁
Vice Chairman	副總裁
President	董事長
Vice President	副董事長
General Manager (GM)	總經理
Vice President (VP)	副總經理
Chief Executive Officer (CEO)	執行長
Chief Financial Officer (CFO)	財務長
Chief Information Officer (CIO)	資訊長
Chief Knowledge Officer (CKO)	知識長
Chief Operating Officer (COO)	營運長
Chief Technology Officer (CTO)	技術長
Consultant	顧問
Adviser	顧問
Special Assistant	特別助理
Factory Chief	廠長

Factory Sub-Chief	副廠長
Director	協理
Assistant Vice President	協理
Director	處長
Vice Director	副處長
Manager	經理
Assistant Manager	副理
Junior Manager	襄理
Section Manager	課長
Deputy Section Manager	副課長
Supervisor	主任
Team Leader	組長
Administrator	管理師
Accountant	會計
Auditor	稽核
Engineer	工程師
Chief Engineer	首席工程師
Advisory Engineer	顧問工程師
Principle Engineer	策劃工程師
System Engineer	系統工程師
Project Leader Engineer	主任工程師
Account Engineer	專案工程師
Senior Engineer	高級工程師
Engineer	工程師
Deputy Engineer	副工程師
Assistant Engineer	助理工程師
Assistant	助理

Clerk	事務員	118
Operator	作業員	
Representative	代表	
Secretary	秘書	
Staff	職員	
senior specialist	高級專員	
Specialist	專員	
Senior Technician	高級技術員	
Technician	技術員	
Assistant Technician	助理技術員	
Team Leader	領班	
Web Master	網站管理專員	
Assistant	助理	
maintenance worker janitor	工友	
contract employee	約聘人員	
messenger	文件遞送員	
volunteer	志工	
temporary worker	臨時人員	
substitute civilian serviceman	替代役男	

258

辦公室各處室

Head Office	總公司
Branch Office	分公司
Chairman's Office	董事長室
Group	事業群
Division	事業處
Department (Dept.)	部門
Administrative Dept.	行政部
Customer Service Dept.	客服部
Finance Dept.	財務部
Financial & Administrative Dept.	管理部
General Affairs Dept.	總務部
Human Resources Dept.	人力資源部
Public Relations	公關
Marketing Dept.	行銷部
Planning Dept.	企劃部
Procurement Dept.	採購部
IT Dept.	資訊部
Computer Center	電腦中心
Quality Control Dept. (QC)	品管部
R&D Dept.	研發部
Legal Dept.	法務部
Sales Dept.	業務部
Auditorial Room	稽核室
Mail Room	收發室

● 辦公室設備

辦公事務機

typewriter	打字機
fax machine	傳真機
photocopier	影印機
copy room	影印室
photocopy	影印
paper shredder	碎紙機
(public) telephone	(公共)電話
answering machine	電話答錄機
scale	磅秤
laminating film	護貝膠膜
battery	電池

辦公傢俱

steel cabinet	鐵櫃
desk	辦公桌
chair	辦公椅
fluorescent light	日光燈
electricity switch	電源開關
ceiling fan	吊扇
fan	電扇
garbage can	垃圾桶
recycle trash can	可回收垃圾桶
wastepaper basket	廢紙簍
vacuum	吸塵器
dehumidifier	除濕機

電腦及週邊

printer	印表機
laser printer	雷射印表機
jet printer	噴墨印表機
scanner	掃描機
toner	碳粉 色帶
PC personal computer	個人電腦
hard disk	硬碟
mouse	滑鼠
hardware	硬體
software	軟體
disk, disc	磁碟片
headphone	耳機
monitor	螢幕 監視器

檔案 / 雜物儲藏室

storage	雜物間
storage	儲藏室 物品儲藏室
warehouse	倉庫
facility room	設備室
tool room	工具室
equipment room	器材室

單字 急救包

盥洗室

restroom	洗手間	(120)
toilet close stool	廁所，馬桶	
stool lid	馬桶蓋	
stool seat	馬桶座	
toilet paper holder	衛生紙架	
toilet paper	衛生紙	
toilet roll	衛生紙滾筒	
water tank	水箱	
soap	肥皂	
soap stand	肥皂台	
mirror	鏡子	
faucet	水龍頭	
tap water	自來水	
water	水	
wash basin sink	洗手台	

機房

phone operator's room	
	總機房
closed-circuit monitor system	
	閉路監視系統
computer facilities	電腦設備，機房
archive	檔案室
archive cabinet	檔案櫃 文書櫃

茶水間 / 休息區

drinking fountain water fountain	飲水機
free water served	茶水供應
water cooler	茶水間
vending machine	自動販賣機
restaurant	餐廳
gym	健身中心
smoking room	吸煙室
smoking area	吸煙區
no smoking	禁止吸煙
convenience shop	福利社
reception room	會客室 接待室 招待室
lounge	休息室 交誼中心
driver's lounge	司機室

消防安全

fire hydrant	消防栓
fire extinguisher	滅火器
escape sling	緩降機
emergency lamp	緊急照明
evacuation route	疏散方向
exit	太平門
emergency exit	安全門

公共空間

bulletin board	公佈欄	
notice board	布告牌	
billboard	佈告欄	
parking lot	停車場	
reserved parking space	專用停車位	
elevator	電梯	
stairs	樓梯	
first floor	一樓	
second floor	二樓	
third floor	三樓	
fourth floor	四樓	
fifth floor	五樓	
sixth floor	六樓	
seventh floor	七樓	
eighth floor	八樓	
ninth floor	九樓	
tenth floor	十樓	
mail box	信箱	
sign	招牌 指標	
umbrella stand umbrella holder	雨傘架	
ATM; automatic teller machine	自動提款機	

會議室

whiteboard	白板
blackboard	黑板
microphone	麥克風
audio-visual materials	視聽器材
overhead projector	投影機
slide projector	幻燈機
transparency	投影片
slide	幻燈片
portable overhead projector	攜帶型投影儀
desktop overhead projector	臺式投影儀
projector screen	投影螢幕
photograph	照片
picture	圖片
transparency	投影片
VCR (video cassette record)	錄放影機
video player	放影機
CD player	CD錄放音機
video tape	錄影帶
remote controller	遙控器
transparency pen	投影筆
whiteboard pen	
marker	白板筆

laser pen	雷射筆	(122)
pointer	指示物	
	指針	
	教鞭	
laser printer	雷射印表機	
electric wire	電線	
outlet	插座	
plug	插頭	
eraser	板擦	
eraser dusting machine		
	板擦機	
gavel	議事槌	
television set	電視機	
AC; Air Conditioner	冷氣	
computer	電腦	
curtain	窗簾	
blind	百葉窗簾	
rostrum	講台	
platform		
public gallery	旁聽席	
briefing room	簡報室	
conference room	會議室	
hall	會堂	
	大廳	

● 書信及電話

書信溝通短語

PLS, PLZ please	請
ASAP as soon as possible	越快越好
LTNS long time no see	好久不見
BTW by the way	順道一提
w/o without	沒有，無
w/, w with	有，和
PPL people	人們，人
FYI for your information	供您參考
OT overtime	加班
POV point of view	觀點
FTR for the record	列入紀錄
spec. specification	規格書
MSG message	訊息

VIT vitamin	維他命	(123)
DIY do it yourself	自己動手做	
dbl double	雙份	
SOP Standard Operating Procedures	標準作業程序	

文具也是辦公室裡常見用品之一喔！為了避免重複，請同時參考生活用品～ 文具用品一節。

書信常用詞彙

address	地址
addressor	寄件人
addressee	收件人
CC; Carbon Copy	抄送
BCC Blind Carbon Copy	密件抄送
company letterhead	印有公司名稱的信箋
bear	印有，寫有
parcel	包裹
correspondence	信件，通信
business correspondence	商業書信
personal correspondence	私人信函
mailbox	郵筒

overweight	超重
postal code	郵地區號
zip code	郵地區號
postcard	明信片
air mail	航空郵寄
ordinary mail	普通郵件
regular mail	
surface mail	
express mail	快遞郵件
registered mail	掛號郵件
register	登記 註冊
sticker	粘膠
stamp	郵票
printed matter	印刷品
delivery	投遞
postman	郵差
seal	封箋
via…	經由…
confidential	機密的
return address	回郵地址
telegram	電報
express telegram	加急電報
urgent telegram	
telegraph office	電報局
per	根據
per your instructions	根據你的指示

電話溝通

disconnect	切斷(電話) (124)
connect	接通(電話)
dial	撥電話
bad connection **poor connection**	訊號不清
busy, engaged	占線
get through **put through**	接通
hang on **hold on**	稍等
take a message	傳話
call back	回電
dial the wrong number **have the wrong number**	撥錯號
caller **initiate(the call)** **originate(the call)**	發話方
caller ID	來電顯示
identify	確認 表明(身分)
speakerphone	免持聽筒
put on speakerphone	將聲音用免持 聽筒放出來
DDD **domestic direct dial**	國內直撥

IDD	國際直撥
international direct dial	
country code	國家代碼
area code	區號
extension	分機
city call	市話
long-distance call	長途電話
emergence call	緊急電話
free call	免費電話
official call	公事電話
private number	私人電話
switchboard	總機
operator	接線生
information	查號臺
cellular phone	行動電話
intercom	對講裝置
walky-talky	無線電對講機
mobile telephone	行動電話
public telephone	公用電話
telephone booth	電話亭
telephone directory	電話薄
beeper	傳呼機
radio paging service	無線傳呼服務台
telephone exchange	交換臺

● 會議英語

會議開始

presentation	表演,介紹 (125)
present agenda	議程
procedure	程序,手續,步驟
order	順序,次序
theme, subject	主題
objective, purpose	目的,目標
topic for discussion	議題,討論的主題
other business	其他事項,臨時動議

會議記錄

to do list	待辦事項
action item	(會議紀錄)事項
task	任務
action plan	行動計畫
outstanding list	未解決的事項
meeting minutes	會議紀律

會議中的爭執

dispute quarrel argument	爭論,爭執
I'm afraid I can't accept	恐怕不能接受
be worried at …	對…感到苦惱
it is difficult to…	難以…
it's not possible to…	無法,不可能
condition	條件

會議常見口語

furnish	供應，提供配置，裝備
whatever	任何種類程度的，無論什麼
whatsoever whatever	whatever 的強勢語氣
modest	保守
liability	責任義務，債務
responsibility	責任
strictly	嚴格的
appreciate	感激謝謝
consider⋯	考量⋯
base on	基於
moreover⋯	再之⋯
unless⋯	除非⋯
subject to	以⋯為準
prior	在先的在前的，前提
be prepared to⋯	準備做⋯事
meet each other half way	折衷一下
make headway	有進展
on the same terms	以同樣條件
limit	底限

請求發言

take the floor	發言 (126)
address the meeting declaration	聲明
statement make a speech	做報告
deliver a speech ask for the floor	要求發言
give the floor to	同意...發言

其他

let me put it this way	換個方式說
I am here today to…	我今天來是為了…
It's my honor to…	很榮幸...
let's begin.	開始吧！
any questions?	有問題嗎？
good question	問得好
share with us	與我們分享
opinion	意見
look into it	進一步研究
get back to you	回答你
disclose	洩漏
confidential	機密

● 評論數據

形容數據合理

acceptable	可以接受
feasible	可行的
workable	
realistic	合乎實際
reasonable	合理
practicable	行得通的
attractive	有吸引力
induce	
convince	
competitive	有競爭力

形容數據不合理

unacceptable	不可接受
infeasible	不可行的
unrealistic	不實際
unreasonable	不合理
impracticable	行不通的
not attractive	無吸引力
not induce	
not convince	
not competitive	無競爭力

下降的數據

weaken	疲軟，削弱 (127) 減弱，減少
turn low fall drop down	下跌
decline	下跌，拒絕
dip	(價格的)下跌
sag	(物價等)下降 下跌，蕭條
plummet	筆直落下
price tobogganed	價格暴跌
decrease	減少
cut down	減價
sudden drop fall rapidly	急降
decrease to fall to drop to	下降到
drop gradually steady decline	逐漸下降
drop slightly	輕微下跌
sharply fall	急劇下跌
fall suddenly	突然下跌
downsizing	縮減
downturn	降低，向下彎曲
downslide	下跌

走勢平穩的數據

hover between...	(數字)徘徊於…
level off	(數字)驅平
easy off	(數字)趨於疲軟
steady	穩固的，平穩的
stable	
remain stable at...	平穩維持在
remain the same	持平
fluctuate around...	在…之間波動
the vibration of...	的波動
remain at	維持在…

上升或逆轉的數據

up	上漲
advance	
turn high	
rise	
raise	
rise perpendicularly	直線上升
skyrocket	猛漲
hike	(猛地)拉，舉，提
shoot up	飛漲
rise in a spiral	螺旋形上升
	不斷加劇地增加
look up	看漲
twice of...	的兩倍
lift (the price)	抬高(價格)

(price) pick up	(價格)回升	128
reach the peak of	到達頂峰…	
increase suddenly	突然增加	
dramatic increase		
increase sharply	急劇上升	
increase steadily	平穩增加	
great increase	大量增加	
significantly exceed	大幅超越	
exceed	超越	
have a great jump	大幅上升	
have a great rise		
jump to		
go up dramatically		
go up	上升	
jump sharply from...	從…激增	
improve	改善 增進 進步	
rise slightly to	輕微上升 慢慢上升	
reverse	逆轉	

First-Aid
Vocabulary

國際金融

● 銀行財會

銀行常用字彙

bank	銀行
bank teller	銀行出納
teller's window	出納櫃檯

帳戶

open an account	開戶
account	帳戶
passbook	存摺
deposit	存款
withdraw	提款

貸款

installment	分期付款
pay by installment	
payment by installment	
monthly payment	按月付款
residential mortgage loan	
	房屋抵押貸款
examining loan	審核貸款
approving loan	批准貸款
floating capital loan	流動資金貸款
commercial lending	經常性貸款
internal audit	內部審核
internal capital allocation	
	內部資金調度

支票

cash a check	兌現支票	(130)
cash	兌現	
promissory note	本票	
bad check	空頭支票	
dishonored check		
rubber check		
endorse	背書	
endorsement		
blank endorse	空白背書	

匯款

remittance	匯款
commercial bill	商業匯票
banker's bill	銀行匯票

支付

dishonor	拒付
payment (n.)	支付
	付款
pay (v.)	付款
	支付
	償還
deferred payment	延期付款

利息

bank interest	銀行利息
interest rate	利率
	匯兌
exchange rate	兌換率
cash	現金
devaluation	貨幣貶值
revaluation	貨幣增值
foreign exchange fluctuation	
	外匯波動
foreign exchange crisis	
	外匯危機
discount	貼現
discount rate	貼現率
bank rate	
financial market	金融市場
international balance of payment	
	國際收支

● 股市經濟

經濟詞彙

inflation	通貨膨脹
deflation	通貨緊縮
economic cycle	經濟周期
economic boom	經濟繁榮
economic recession	經濟衰退

economic depression	經濟蕭條 (131)
economic crisis	經濟危機
economic recovery	經濟復甦
bubble economy	泡沫經濟
overheating of economy	經濟過熱
macro economy	宏觀經濟
favorable balance	順差
adverse balance	逆差
slump	不景氣
recession	衰退
growth rate	成長率
average growth rate	均成長率
rate of return on investment	投資報酬率
total foreign trade value	外貿進出口總額
improve economic performance	提高經濟效益
increase economic return	提高經濟效益
risk rating	風險評等
attract investment	吸引投資
private sector	民間機構 私人機構
supporting policy	配套政策
technology intensive	技術密集

labor intensive	勞動密集
mass production	大規模生產
market capitalization	市場資本總額
risk management	風險管理
mutual fund	共同基金

股市債券

public bond	公債
stock, share	股票
debenture	債券
stock exchange	股票交易所
allotment of share	配股
the main board	主板市場
the second board market	二板市場
stock market	股票市場
list on the stock market	股票上市
stock index	股市指數
IPO Initial Public Offering	首次上市

● 世界金融

亞洲貨幣簡稱

TWD ; dollar	台幣
JPY ; yen	日元
THB ; baht	泰國銖

MYR；ringgit	馬來西亞林吉特
RMB；renminbi yuan	人民幣
HKD；dollar	港幣
MOP；pataca	澳門元
PHP；peso	菲律賓批索
SGD；dollar	新加坡元
IRR；rial	伊朗里亞爾
KWD；dinar	科威特第納爾
RS；rupee	印度盧比

非洲貨幣簡稱

ZAR；rand	南非蘭特
DZD；dinar	阿爾及利亞第納爾
EGP；pound	埃及磅
MAD；dirham	摩洛哥迪拉姆
AON；new kwanza	安哥拉寬扎
TND；dinar	突尼西亞第納爾

美洲貨幣簡稱

CAD；dollar	加拿大元
USD；dollar	美元

歐洲貨幣簡稱

EUR；euro	歐元	
FRF；franc	法國法郎	
DEM；mark	德國馬克	
ITL；lira	義大利里拉	
NLG；guilder	荷蘭基爾德	
BEF；franc	比利時法郎	
LUF；franc	盧森堡法郎	
IEP；pound	愛爾蘭鎊	
ESP；peseta	西班牙比賽塔	
FIM；markka	芬蘭馬克	
ATS；schilling	奧地利先令	
DKK；krone	丹麥克朗	
SEK；krone	瑞典克朗	
NOK；krone	挪威克朗	
CHF；franc	瑞士法郎	
GBP；pound	英鎊	

澳洲貨幣簡稱

UD；dollar	澳大利亞元
NZD；dollar	紐西蘭元

澳洲股市指數

Australia All Ordinaries

澳洲雪梨普通股指數

重要經濟指標

economic indicators	經濟指標	
exchange rates	匯率	
lending rates	借款利率	
GDP growth rates	經濟成長率	
unemployment rates	失業率	
per capital GDP	平均每人 GDP	

CPI; consumer price index
消費者物價指數

foreign exchange reserves
外匯存底

industrial output growth rates
工業生產增加率

GDP; gross domestic product
國內生產毛額

GNP; gross national product
國民生產毛額

RPI; retail price index
零售物價指數

歐洲股市指數

Argentina Merval
阿根廷股票指數

Copenhagen Stock Exchange
丹麥哥本哈根證交所指數

DAX (30 stocks)
德國法蘭克福 **DAX** 指數

DJ Euro STOXX 50
道瓊歐盟 50 指數

FTSE 100
英國倫敦金融時報百種指數

France CAC 40
法國巴黎證商公會 40 種指數

Belgium Bel20 Index
比利時布魯塞爾 BEL20 指數

ATX (Austria)
奧地利 ATX 指數

Brazil BOVESPA (Sao Paolo)
巴西聖保羅 BOVESPA 指數

Amsterdam Exchanges (AEX)
荷蘭阿姆斯特丹 AEX 指數

Madrid Stock Exchange
西班牙馬德里證交所指數

Italian MIBTEL
義大利米蘭 MIBTEL 指數

美洲股市指數

AMEX Composite
美國 AMEX 指數

AMEX Oil & Gas Index
AMEX 石油暨天然氣指數

Dow Jones Industrials
美國紐約道瓊工業指數

Dow Jones Utilities
美國道瓊公用事業指數

NASDAQ
(National Association of Securities Dealers Automated Quotation)
納斯達克（高技術企業板）

Canada TSE 300 Composite
加拿大多倫多 **300** 種綜合指數

Mexico Share Index
墨西哥 **IPC** 股票指數

亞洲股市指數

Bombay BSE SENSEX
印度孟買 **30** 種指數

Hong Kong Hang Seng
香港恆生指數

Jakarta SE Index
印尼雅加達證交所指數

Korea SE Composite
韓國漢城綜合指數

Malaysia KLSE Composite
馬來西亞吉隆坡證交所指數

Manila Composite
菲律賓馬尼拉綜合指數

● 國家及首都

國家；首都(A-Z)

Afghanistan；Kabul
阿富汗；喀布爾

Albania；Tirana
阿爾巴尼亞；地拉那

Algeria；Algiers
阿爾及利亞；阿爾及爾

United States of America；Washington DC
美國；華盛頓

Angola；Luanda
安哥拉；魯安達

Argentina；Buenos Aires
阿根廷；布宜諾斯艾利斯

Armenia；Yerevan
亞美尼亞；葉里溫

Australia；Canberra
澳大利亞；坎培拉

Austria；Vienna
奧地利；維也納

Azerbaijan；Baku
亞塞拜然；巴庫

Bahamas；Nassau
巴哈馬；拿騷

Belarus；Minsk
白俄羅斯；明斯克

Belgium ; Brussels (135)
比利時；布魯塞爾

Belize ; Belmopan
貝里斯；貝爾墨邦

Bhutan ; Thimphu
不丹；辛布

Bolivia ; La Paz
玻利維亞；拉巴斯

Brazil ; Brasilia
巴西；巴西利亞

Brunei ; Bandar Seri Begawan
汶萊；斯里貝加萬市

Bulgaria ; Sofia
保加利亞；索菲亞

Cambodia ; Phnom Penh
柬埔寨；金邊

Canada ; Ottawa
加拿大；渥太華

Central African Republic ; Bangui
中非；班基

People's Republic of China ; Beijing
中華人民共和國；北京

Colombia ; Bogotá
哥倫比亞；波哥大

Croatia ; Zagreb
克羅埃西亞；札格拉布

Cuba ; Havana
古巴；哈瓦那

Republic of Cyprus ; Nicosia
賽普勒斯；尼古西亞

Czech Republic ; Prague
捷克;布拉格

Denmark ; Copenhagen
丹麥;哥本哈根

Dominica ; Roseau
多米尼克;羅梭

Dominican Republic ; Santo Domingo
多明尼加;聖多明哥

Ecuador ; Quito
厄瓜多;基多

Egypt ; Cairo
埃及;開羅

El Salvador ; San Salvador
薩爾瓦多;聖薩爾瓦多

Equatorial Guinea ; Malabo
赤道幾內亞;馬拉波

Estonia ; Tallinn
愛沙尼亞;塔林

Fiji ; Suva
斐濟;蘇瓦

Finland ; Helsinki
芬蘭;赫爾辛基

France ; Paris
法國;巴黎

Gambia ; Banjul
甘比亞;班竹市

Georgia ; Tbilisi
喬治亞;提比利西

Germany ; Berlin
德國;柏林

Greece；Athens (136)
希臘；雅典

Guatemala；Guatemala City
瓜地馬拉；瓜地馬拉市

Holy See or Vatican；Vatican City
教廷 or 梵蒂岡；梵蒂岡城

Honduras；Tegucigalpa
宏都拉斯；德古斯加巴

Hungary；Budapest
匈牙利；布達佩斯

Iceland；Reykjavik
冰島；雷克雅維克

India；New Delhi
印度；新德里

Indonesia；Jakarta
印尼；雅加達

Iran；Tehran
伊朗；德黑蘭

Iraq；Baghdad
伊拉克；巴格達

Ireland；Dublin
愛爾蘭；都柏林

Israel；Jerusalem
以色列；耶路撒冷

Italy；Rome
義大利；羅馬

Jamaica；Kingston
牙買加；京斯敦

Japan；Tokyo
日本；東京

Jordan ; Amman
約旦;安曼

Kazakhstan ; Astana
哈薩克;阿斯塔納

Kenya ; Nairobi
肯亞;奈洛比

North Korea ; Pyongyang
北韓;平壤

South Korea ; Seoul
韓國;首爾

Kuwalt ; Kuwait City
科威特;科威特市

Laos ; Vientiane
寮國;永珍

Latvia ; Riga
拉脱維亞;里加

Lebanon ; Belrut
黎巴嫩;貝魯特

Liberia ; Monrovia
賴比瑞亞;蒙羅維亞

Libya ; Tripoli
利比亞;的黎波里

Lithuania ; Vilnius
立陶宛;維爾紐斯

Luxembourg ; Luxembourg City
盧森堡;盧森堡城

Madagascar ; Antananarivo
馬達加斯加;安塔那那利佛

Malaysia ; Kuala Lumpur
馬來西亞;吉隆坡

Maldives ; Male
馬爾地夫;馬列

Malta ; Valletta
馬爾他;瓦勒他

Mauritius ; Port Louis
模里西斯;路易士港

Mexico ; Mexico City
墨西哥;墨西哥城

Macedonia, F.Y.R.O. ; Skopje
馬其頓;史可普列

Marshall Islands ; Majuro
馬紹爾群島;馬久羅

Monaco ; Monaco
摩納哥;摩納哥城

Mongolia ; Ulaanbaatar
蒙古;烏蘭巴托

Morocco ; Rabat
摩洛哥;拉巴特

Mozambique ; Maputo
莫三比克;馬布多

Myanmar ; Rangoon
緬甸;賓馬拿

Nepal ; Katmandu
尼泊爾;加德滿都

Netherlands ; Amsterdam
荷蘭;阿姆斯特丹

New Zealand ; Wellington
紐西蘭;威靈頓

Nicaragua ; Managua
尼加拉瓜;馬拿瓜

Nigeria；Abuja
奈及利亞；阿布札

Norway；Oslo
挪威；奧斯陸

Oman；Muscat
阿曼；馬斯喀特

Pakistan；Islamabad
巴基斯坦；伊斯蘭瑪巴德

Palau；Koror
帛琉；科羅爾

Palestine；Jerusalem
巴勒斯坦；耶路撒冷

Panama；Panama City
巴拿馬；巴拿馬城

Paraguay；Asuncion
巴拉圭；亞松森

Peru；Lima
秘魯；利馬

Philippines；Manila
菲律賓；馬尼拉

Poland；Warsaw
波蘭；華沙

Portugal；Lisbon
葡萄牙；里斯本

Puerto Rico；San Juan
波多黎各；聖胡安

Republic of the Congo；Brazzaville
剛果共和國；布拉薩

Romania；Bucharest
羅馬尼亞；布加勒斯特

Russia ; Moscow (138)
俄羅斯；莫斯科

Saudi Arabia ; Riyadh
沙烏地阿拉伯；利雅德

Singapore ; Singapore City
新加坡；新加坡

Slovakia ; Bratislava
斯洛伐克；布拉提斯拉瓦

South Africa ; Bloemfontein
南非；普利托里亞(行政)

South Africa ; Cape Town
南非；開普敦(立法)

South Africa ; Pretoria
南非；布隆泉(司法)

Spain ; Madrid
西班牙；馬德里

Sri Lanka ; Colombo
斯里蘭卡；可倫坡

Sudan ; Khartoum
蘇丹；喀土穆

Sweden ; Stockholm
瑞典；斯德哥爾摩

Switzerland ; Bern
瑞士；伯恩

Syria ; Damascus
敘利亞；大馬士革

Taiwan ; Taipei
臺灣；台北

Thailand ; Bangkok
泰國；曼谷

Trinidad and Tobago ; Port-of-Spain
千里達及托巴哥;西班牙港

Tunisia ; Tunis
突尼西亞;突尼斯

Turkey ; Ankara
土耳其;安卡拉

Tuvalu ; Funafuti
吐瓦魯;福納佛提

Ukraine ; Kiev
烏克蘭;基輔

United Arab Emirates ; Abu Dhabi
阿拉伯聯合大公國;阿布達比

United Kingdom ; London
英國;倫敦

Uruguay ; Montevideo
烏拉圭;蒙特維多

Uzbekistan ; Tashkent
烏茲別克;塔什干

Venezuela ; Caracas
委內瑞拉;卡拉卡斯

Vietnam ; Hanoi
越南;河內

● 世界重要機關及城市

世界重要機關別名

Big Board	大行情板, 紐約證券交易 (139)
Wall Street	華爾街, 美國金融市場
Madison Avenue	麥迪遜大街 美國廣告業中心
Capitol Hill	美國國會
Foggy Bottom 諷刺發言人的發言經常模糊不清	霧谷,美國國務院
Pentagon, Penta	五角大樓, 美國國防部
Film Capital of the World **Hollywood**	世界影都,好萊塢
Broadway	百老匯大街
Uncle Sam	山姆大叔, 縮寫剛好是 **U.S.** 指美國政府或美國人
Fleet Street	佛里特街, 英國新聞界
the City	英國首都倫敦市 指英國商業金融界
Scotland Yard	福爾摩斯小說裡的 蘇格蘭場亦指倫敦 警方
White House	白宮,指美國政府 或總統本人

Buckingham Palace
英國白金漢宮，英國皇室

Elysee
法國總統官邸，泛指法國政府

No.10 Downing Street
唐寧街 10 號，英國首相官邸

Quai d'Orsay
凱道賽碼頭
法國外交部所在地名，亦指法國政府

美國州名別稱

Golden State, California
黃金州，加利福尼亞

Sunshine State, Florida
陽光州，佛羅里達

Keystone State, Pennsylvania
賓夕法尼亞，拱石州

Lone Star State, Texas
孤星州，德克薩斯

Buckeye State, Ohio
七葉樹州，俄亥俄

Green Mountain State, Vermont
佛蒙特，翠巒州

Empire State, New York
帝國州，紐約州

Land of Lincoln, Illinois
林肯的故鄉，美國伊利諾州

Mother of Presidents, Virginia
總統之母，美國維吉尼亞州

Evergreen State, Washington (140)
常青州，華盛頓

Sunflower State, Kansas
向日葵州，堪薩斯

Aloha State, Hawaii
阿囉哈州，夏威夷

Constitution State, Connecticut
憲法州，康乃迪克

**Centennial State,
Silver State, Colorado**
百年州，銀州，科羅拉多

Bluegrass State, Kentucky
牧草州，肯塔基

Free State, Maryland
自由州，馬利蘭

Mountain State, Montana
山嶽州，蒙大拿

Magnolia State, Mississippi
木蘭花州，密西西比

Pine Tree State, Maine
松樹州，緬因

Great Lakes State, Michigan
大湖州，密西根

美國大城市的別名

**Beantown, Hub of the Universe,
Boston**
豆城，宇宙中心，美國波士頓市

Big Apple, Fun City, New York
大蘋果，逍遙城，紐約市

City of Angels, Los Angeles
天使城，洛杉磯

Windy City, Chicago
多風城，芝加哥市

City of Brotherly Love, Philadelphia
博愛城，費城

City by the Golden Gate, San Francisco
金門城，三藩市

Motor City, Motown, Detroit
汽車城，底特律市

Crescent City, New Orleans
新月城，新奧爾良市

Dice City, Las Vegas
賭城，拉斯維加斯市

Steel City, Pittsburgh
鋼城，匹茲堡市

Bison City, Buffalo
野牛城，布法羅，水牛城

英國大城市別名

Peanut City, Suffolk
花生城，英國一郡名，薩福克

Pittsburgh of the South, Birmingham
英國一城市名伯明翰，南方鋼都

● 報紙要聞

新聞報導

on-the-spot broadcasting (141)	
	現場直播
televise	實況轉播
on-the-spot interview	
	現場採訪
news flash	短訊
	快訊
folo follow-up	連續報導
in-depth reporting	深度報導
interpretative reporting	
	解釋性報導
investigative reporting	
	調查性報導
quarters, circles	…界
educational circles	教育界
judicial circles	司法界
press circles	新聞界
political circles	政治界
literary and art circles	
	藝文界
entertainment circles	
	娛樂圈
show-biz	演藝界

刊物分類

carry	刊登
daily	日報
weekly	週報
monthly	月刊
bi-monthly	雙月刊
quarterly	季刊
periodical	期刊
journal	期刊
newspaper	報紙
evening paper	晚報
morning paper	晨報
popular paper	大眾化報紙
digest	文摘
magazine	雜誌
tabloid	小報，以報導轟動話題為主
popular paper	大眾化報紙
quality paper	內容較嚴肅的報紙
medium	媒體，媒介
media	媒介，媒體 (複數)
mass communication	大眾傳播學
mass media	大眾傳播媒介

新聞版面

around the world	國際新聞版	(142)
entertainment	娛樂版	
tourism	旅遊專版	
financial section	(報刊的) 金融版	
domestic news	國內新聞	
stocks	股市版	
lifestyle	生活版	
supplement	副刊 增刊	
editorial	社論	
focus	新聞聚焦	
banner	橫幅標題	
flag	報頭 報名	
master head	報頭 報名	
top news	頭條新聞	
front page	頭條	
subhead	小標題 副標題	
lead	導語，導讀	
highlights	要聞	
brief	簡訊	
bulletin	新聞簡報	
documents	文件摘要	
essay	隨筆	

相關人員

contributing editor	特約編輯
accredited journalist	特派記者
stringer	特約記者 通訊員
correspondent	駐外記者 常駐外埠記者
journalist	新聞記者
cameraman	攝影記者
reporter	記者
columnist	專欄作家
free-lancer	自由撰稿人 自由業者
contributor	投稿人
PR, public relationship	公關(人員)

編輯

editor	編輯
copy editor	文字編輯
proofreader	校對員
remuneration	稿費
publisher	出版者
layout	版面編排
makeup	版面設計
caption	圖片說明
faxed photo	傳真照片

商業財經	
biz	商業 (143)
business	商業
knowledge economy	知識經濟
economic take-off	經濟起飛
economic sanction	經濟制裁
climb out	經濟復甦
bottom out	走出低谷
bubble economy	泡沫經濟
floor trader	場內交易人
operating margin	營運利潤
shortfall	不足，差額，赤字
hedge-fund	對沖基金
anti-trust	反托拉斯
balance sheet	資產負債表
borrower	債方
inventory	貨存、庫存量
mutual fund	共同基金
active capital	流動資本
active trade balance	順差
adverse trade balance	逆差
daily turnover	日成交量
closing price	收盤價
stake	股份，利害關係
black market price	黑市價
boycott	聯合抵制

boost	增加，提高
boom	(經濟)繁榮 興旺
soar	急劇上升
ceiling price	最高限價
lop	下降，減少
dip	下降
axe	解雇，減少
plunge	價格等暴跌
plummet	價格等暴跌
trim	削減
ease	減輕，緩和
end	結束，中止
terminate	結束，中止
freeze	凍結，平穩
bottle up	抑制
glut	供過於求
supply-demand imbalance	供求失調
bid up price	哄抬物價
financial quarters	金融界方面
long-term，low-interest loan	長期低息貸款
interest-free loan	無息貸款
inflation-proof deposit	保值儲蓄
trustee	董事
tycoon	巨富

highly-sophisticated technology (144)	
	尖端技術
redundant	失業人員
re-employment	二次就業
laid-off	失業，下崗
in-service training	在職訓練
brawn drain	勞工外流
brain drain	人才流失
brain gain	人才引進
labor-management conflict	
	勞資衝突
richly-paid job	薪水豐厚的工作
hand-to-mouth pay	溫飽工資
on-the-job training	在職培訓
overstaff	人員過多
lift an embargo	解除禁運
embargo	禁運，封港
all-out ban	全面禁止
crude output	原油生產
crude oil	原油
APEC; Asia-Pacific Economic Cooperation	亞太經合組織
OPEC; Organization Of Petroleum Exporting Countries	石油輸出國組織
WTO; World Trade Organization	世界貿易組織
GATT; General Agreement On Tariffs And Trade	關貿總協定

社會要聞

criminal law	刑法
con; convict	罪犯
counselor	律師
case	案件
lawyer	律師
solicitor	初級律師
defendant	被告
acquit	宣告…無罪 無罪釋放
guilty	有罪的
innocent	無罪的
abduct	誘拐 綁架
big lie	大騙局
rip off	偷竊
arson	放火 縱火
professional escort	特種服務
escort girl	伴遊女郎
poverty-stricken area	貧困地區
hit-and-runner	肇事後逃逸者
hit and run	肇事逃逸
pedestrian	行人
passerby	過路人
heroin	海洛因
witnesses	證人 目擊者

nab, arrest	逮捕	(145)
hold	逮捕	
slay, murder	謀殺	
fake	贗品	
	騙局	
laud, praise	讚揚	
bare, expose	暴露	
reveal	揭露	
assail, denounce	譴責	
denunciation	譴責、指責	
black box	測謊器	
porn; pornography	情色	
accuse	控告	
charge	控告	
sentence	判刑	
death penalty	死刑	
capital punishment	死刑	
air crash	飛機失事	
crash; collision	碰撞，墜毀	
pseudo event	假新聞	
invasion of privacy	侵犯隱私權	
libel	誹謗罪	
frame-up	誣陷，陷害	
public opinion	輿論	
imported red fire ant	入侵紅火蟻	
flay	批評	
rap	批評	

rebuke	批評
criticize	批評
suspended interest	懷疑 懸念
eye-account	目擊記， 記者見聞
skeleton in the closet	見不得人的秘密
Achilles' heel	(唯一的)致命傷， 弱點
chute parachute	降落傘
copter helicopter chopper	直升機
flying squad	機動小組
flout insult	侮辱
rift separation	隔離 分離
clash	發生分歧 爭議
curb	控制
check examine	檢查
grill nvestigate probe	調查
plot conspire	預謀，密謀策劃

醫藥新聞

depression	憂鬱症	(146)
cancer	癌症	
evacuate	使(人)撤離	
SARS; severe acute respiratory syndrome	嚴重的急性的呼吸的症候群	
fatal	致命的	
break out	爆發	
virus	病毒	
quarantine	隔離	
isolate	隔離 孤立	
plague	疫病	
epidemic	流行病 傳染的	
contagion	接觸傳染	
aerial infection	空氣傳染	
bird flu	禽流感	
flu, influenza	流行性感冒	
virus	病毒	
domestic poultry	家禽	
outbreaks	爆發	
migrating	(鳥的)定期移棲 遷徙	
monitoring	監視 追蹤 (鳥的行蹤)	
bacteria	細菌	

國際外交要聞

coup plotter	政變策劃者
dictatorship	獨裁
one-man government	獨裁政府
appropriate authorities	有關當局
peace saboteur	和平破壞者
interim government	過渡政府
bloodless coup	不流血政變
hostage	人質
curfew	宵禁，戒嚴
blockade	封鎖
apartheid	種族隔離
racial discrimination	種族歧視
blast	爆炸
explosion, explode	爆炸
abortive coup attempt	政變未遂
missile	飛彈
SALT; Strategic Arms Limitation Talks 限制戰略武器會談	
SDI; Strategic Defense Initiative 戰略防禦措施	
atomic nucleus	原子核
nuclear weapon	核子武器
atomic weapon	原子武器
denuclearization (使國家或地區)非核化	
armed intervention	武裝干涉

bombard	轟炸，炮擊 (147)
truce	停火，休戰
ceasefire	停火
rout	擊潰，打垮
oust, expel	驅逐
raid, attack	進攻
head, direct	率領
gut, destroy	摧毀
nip, defeat	擊敗
pullout, withdrawal	撤退，撤離
strife, conflict	衝突，矛盾
feud	嚴重分歧
dispute	嚴重分歧
row, quarrel	爭論，爭議
clash; controversy	爭議
hawk	主戰派份子
dove	主和派份子，和平鴿
protocol	草案，協議
map	制訂
work out	制訂
pact	條約
agreement, treaty	條約，協議
deal, agreement	協定
fair-trade agreement	互惠貿易協定
transaction	交易

316

聯合國

UN; United Nations	聯合國
permanent member	常任理事國
allied powers	同盟國
axis power	軸心國
peaceful co-existence	和平共處
peace-keeping force	維和部隊

外交新聞

guest of honor	貴賓
reciprocal visits	互訪
amicable relations	友好關係
face-to-face talk	會晤
top-level talk	高峰會談
arm-twisting	施加壓力
foreign ministry spokesman	外交部發言人
ambassador	大使
ambassadress	大使夫人
envoy	大使
ties; relations	外交關係
bluff diplomacy	恫嚇外交
diplomacy	外交
21-gun salute	**21** 響禮炮
red-carpet welcome	隆重歡迎
honor guard	儀隊

選舉新聞

president	總統	(148)
PM; Prime Minister	總理，首相	
vice president	副總統	
acting president	代總統	
PM; prime minister	首相，總理	
administration party	執政黨	
party in power	執政黨	
party in opposition	在野黨	
conservative party	保守黨	
assembly hall	會議廳	
senate	參議院	
parliament	國會	
body, committee c'tee	組織，委員會	
One-country-two-system policy		
	一國兩制的政策	
anarchy	無政府狀態	
overwhelming majority	壓倒性多數	
negative vote	反對票	
positive vote	贊成票	
roll-call vote	點名投票	
voting card	投票卡	
voting observer	監票員	
speaker	議長	
deputy speraker	副議長	
congressman	國會議員	

congressman	男國會議員
congresswoman	女國會議員
senator	參議員
mayor	市長
incumbent mayor	現任市長
county magistrate	縣長
township head	鄉長
village master	村長
town master	鎮長
rep; representative	代表
politician	政客
tenure of office	任職期
township enterprises	鄉鎮企業
press spokesman	新聞發言人
spokesman	發言人
civilian	平民
cabinet re-shuffle	內閣改組
cabinet lineup	內閣陣容
brain trust	智囊團
official	官員
bureaucrat	官僚
bureaucracy	官僚主義
bribery	行賄
amnesty	特赦
blanket ballot	全面選舉
poll, election	投票選舉
	民意測驗

nominee	候選人 (149)
constituency	選區
	選民
ballot	選票
	投票
arch-foe	主要的勁敵
vow	決心
	發誓
step down	辭職
	下臺
depose	罷免
anti-corruption	反腐敗
presidential election	總統選舉
inaugural address	就職演說
bullet	子彈
name, appoint	命名
	提名
nominate	命名
	提名
election	選舉
ballot	選票
text message	文字簡訊
plebiscite, referendum	公投
purchase arms	購買武器
anti-secession law	反分裂法
independence	獨立
reunification	統一
assassinate	暗殺(行刺)

人物特寫

profile	人物特寫 人物專訪
man of mark	名人 要人
man of the year	年度風雲人物
come out	出櫃 承認是同性戀
come out of the closet	出櫃 承認是同性戀
homosexual	同性戀的正式說法
homo	同性戀
gay	男同性戀
queer, fairy, queen	男同性戀， 較輕蔑的說法
lesbian	女同性戀
heterosexism	異性戀主義者
gay liberation	同性戀解放運動
women's liberation	婦女解放運動
campaign against porns	掃黃運動
enlisted man	現役軍人
big gun	有勢力的人 名人

娛樂體育

show biz	娛樂產業 演藝圈 (150)
affair	桃色新聞 緋聞
sex scandal	桃色新聞
hype	炒作
bistro	夜總會
the other man (woman)	第三者
his-and-hers watches	情侶表
sidebar	相關花絮
pix; pictures	電影
premiere	首映 初次公演
box office returns	票房收入
curtain call	謝幕
closing address	閉幕致辭
box office smash	賣座率高的演出
telly; television	電視機
audience rating	收視率
com'l; commercial	商業的 廣告
DJ; disc jockey	電台節目主持人
album	專輯
chart	(流行音樂)排行榜

hit parade	流行歌曲排行榜
cover girl	封面女郎
crusade	宣傳攻勢
celebrity	名人
	名流
leading actor	男主角
leading actress	女主角
supporting actress	女配角
supporting actor	男配角
invitation meet	邀請賽
knock-out system	淘汰制
eliminate	淘汰
karate	空手道
judo	柔道
guest team	客隊
home team	主隊
ace, champion	得勝者
	冠軍
champ	冠軍
sport	運動
archery	射箭術
archer	射手
taekwondo	跆拳道
dash	短跑
medal	獎牌
umpire	裁判
rapport	默契

分類廣告

obituary	訃告	(151)
advertisement	廣告	
correction	更正(啟事)	
classified ads	分類廣告	
ads (advertisement)	廣告	

報導新聞常用動詞 – 承認

acknowledge	承認
concede	承認
confess	供認，承認
admit	承認
affirm	肯定，確認

報導新聞常用動詞 – 補充

add	接著說，又說
continue	接著說
go on	繼續說，接著說

報導新聞常用動詞 – 宣布／聲稱

proclaim	宣告，聲明
allege	宣稱
declare	聲明聲稱
claim	聲稱
announce	宣佈
state	聲明，聲稱
assert	斷言，聲稱

報導新聞常用動詞 - 告誡

caution	告誡
warn	警告 告誡
remind	提醒 告誡
tip	暗示 告誡
alert	警告
advise	勸告
signal	打信號示意
threaten	威脅 警告
notify	通知 告知

報導新聞常用動詞 - 反駁／爭辯

contradict	反駁 否定
refute	反駁
deny	否認
object	提出異議 反對
protest	抗議
contend	爭辯
argue	主張 爭辯

報導新聞常用動詞 - 評論分析

observe	評述	(152)
remark	評論	
elaborate	詳細述說	
emphasize	詳述 闡明	
analyze	分析道	
suggest	建議	
imply	暗示	
urge	敦促 力勸	

報導新聞常用動詞 - 透露／談及

reveal	透露
disclose	透露
say	說
note	談及 表明
tell	告訴 告知
reply	回答

報導新聞常用動詞 - 闡明主張

maintain	主張 認為
insist	堅持說 主張
reaffirm	重申
reiterate	重申

stress	著重説 強調
emphasize	強調

報導新聞常用動詞 — 其他

boast	誇口
exclaim	大聲説 呼喊
conclude	斷定 下結論
explain	解釋
complain	抱怨
pledge	保證

Chapter

8

新鮮人專區

口語報告
書面報告
應徵面試
不同職缺常用單字
校園稱謂
學校制度
科系課程
校園生活

● 口語報告

逐項說明

the first thing	第一點	(153)
the first point		
in the first place		
the second	第二	
the third	第三	
first	第一	
second	第二	
third	第三	
firstly	第一	
secondly	第二	
thirdly	第三	
step one	第一步	
step two	第二步	
step three	第三步	
the final step	最後一步	
I will start with	我會從…開始	
to begin with	首先	
I will open with...	我會從…開始	
Let's get to…	我們看到…	
I am going to consider…		
	我們談到…	
on our agenda	議程上	
the following days	接下來幾天	

		(154)
following that the next next	接下來	
my next point is	下一點	
then	然後	
after that another	再來	
later on	等一下	
move on to...	談到下一項	
move on	繼續	
let's turn to let's move along to the upcoming	我們談到	
regarding	關於	
previously	事先 以前	
last finally at last the last the final	最後	
to close at the end, wrap up with	結論，總結	

優先權考量

priority	優先，重點 優先權
high priority	最優先考慮
top priority	最高優先權

表達同意 / 贊成

I agree...	我同意…
I think xxx is right.	我認為 xxx 是對的。
I quite agree	我很贊成…

表達不同意 / 不贊成

Unfortunately,...	不幸地，…
I don't agree	我不贊成…
I am not able to…	我無法…
I refuse to...	我拒絕…
I disagree...	我不同意…
I am unable to…	我無法

說明研究結果

based on our survey...	根據我們的調查…
our research shows that...	我們的研究顯示…
the figure reveals...	這數字顯示… 這圖顯示…
we also noticed…	我們也注意到了

as you see... (155)
如各位所見…

base on the conclusion...
根據(我們的)結論…

並列／同等關係

either..., or	任一
neither....,nor	兩者都不
both..., and	兩者都
both	兩者
and	和
as well as	
or	或
not only...., but also	不但…而且
at the same time	同時

表示時間

before	在…之前
after	在…之後
among...	在…之中 在…中間
meanwhile **meantime in the meantime** **at the same time**	同時
while **when** **during** **as**	當…，在…期間

增強語氣

definitely	絕對
indeed	的確
surely	當然
absolutely	絕對
at no time	決不
every single	每一(強調語氣)
under any circumstances	任何情況
in any case	無論如何
whatever happens	不管發生什麼事
anyhow	無論如何
in any event	無論如何
in fact	事實上
to tell the truth frankly speaking	老實説

附加關係

moreover	加之 此外
furthermore	再者
what's more	還有
as well	也 同樣
further	進一步
in addition additionally	額外的 另外

extra	額外的 外加的	(156)
also too	也	
especially	尤其是	
likewise in the same manner in the same way	同樣的	
in addition to...	另外…， 除了…	
except...	除了…	
besides	除…之外	
again	再一次	
along with	與…在一起	
include	包含	

一般而言

on the whole in general	一般而言， 整體而言
in particular... especially....	特別是…
on average,...	平均而言，…
generally speaking	一般來說
as a rule	通常
every	每一
some	一些

most	大多
in most cases	大多數情況下
mainly...	主要是…

回顧，回到先前議題

review	回顧
go over	温習
get back	回到
return	
previous discussion	先前的討論
pick up	繼續 恢復

發生頻率

always	總是 發生機率 **100%**
all the time	總是 發生機率 **100%**
usually	慣常 發生機率 **90%**
frequently	經常 發生機率 **80%**
generally	一般而言 發生機率 **80%**
often	時常 發生機率 **70%**

	(157)
sometimes	有時 發生機率 **50%**
occasionally	有時 發生機率 **40%**
seldom	很少 發生機率 **10%**
rarely	很少，難得 發生機率 **10%**
hardly	幾乎不 發生機率 **5%**
hardly ever	幾乎從不 發生機率 **1%**
never	從不 發生機率 **0%**

發生可能性

definitely	絕對地 可能性 **100%**
absolutely	絕對地 可能性 **100%**
certainly	當然 可能性 **100%**
probably	可能 可能性 **95%**以上
likely	可能 可能性 **95%**以上
possibly	可能 可能性 **50%**

perhaps	大概
	可能性 **20%**
maybe	也許
	可能性 **10%**，也屬
	於較客氣的語氣。

● 書面報告

原因

for	因為
as	
because of	
due to	
on account of	由於
owing to	
since	既然，因為
now that	既然
the main reason is,..	主要原因是，…
for the sake of	因為…緣故
	為了

建議 / 提議

proposal	提案
propose	提議
	建議
	提出
recommendation	忠告
	建議

		(158)
recommend	建議	
suggest		
suggestion		
make suggestion	提出建議	
advocate	提倡	
	擁護者	
nominate	提名	

比較

compare with	與…相比
in comparison with	
likewise	同樣的
in like manner	
in the same way	
similarly	相似的

目的

in order to	為了要
for the purpose of	為…目的
for this purpose	
to this end	為這個目的
with this in mind	
the purpose is	目的是
so that	以致於
	以便

評估

evaluate	評估
feasibility	可行性
specific issue	具體的問題
consider	考慮 考量
survey	調查
preliminary	初步的

轉折

on the one hand	一部分
on the other hand	另一部分
on the contrary	相反的
to the opposite	相對的
in contrast to	
nevertheless	然而
while	
yet	
however	
whereas	反之
instead	反而 卻
but	可是
otherwise	否則
although	雖然

		(159)
though **in spite of** **despite**	儘管	
rather	到不如…, 寧可	
unfortunately	不幸地	
unless...	除非…	

討論

discuss **comment**	討論
further discussion	進一步討論
make a few comments **make a few remarks**	作一些評論
mentioned earlier	先前提到
talk later	等一下談
mention	提到,説起

舉例

for example **for instance** **to illustrate** **i.e. (=id est)** **such as**	舉例來説,譬如説
let's take ... for example **take ... as an example**	讓我們以…為例

an example of this is...	有一個例子是…

總結、歸納

to sum up	總結
summarize	
to conclude	
all in all	總的來說
in short	簡言之，總之
in a word	
in sum	
in consequence	結果
in conclusion	
in brief	簡言之
consequently	因而
on the whole	整體而言
it amounts to the same thing	
	結果相同
as a result	結果，所以，因而
therefore	
thus	
so	
hence	
resolution	決議
outcome	決策
decision	
final confirmation	最後確認
look forward to...	希望…
respond to ...	回覆…

pass on	傳遞	(160)
	轉交	

重申／進一步說明

in the words of...	套用…的話説
in other words	換句話説
put it another way	
that is	那就是
that is to say	
expanding on that,...	
elaborate on...	詳細來説，…
or rather	更確切的説
the point is...	重點是…
take a closer look at...	
	更進一步來看…

● 應徵面試

描述績效表現

accomplish	完成
	成就
implement	實施
achievement	工作成就
	業績
succeed	成功
break the record	打破記錄
participate in	參加
adapted to	適應於

behave	表現
demonstrate	證明，示範操作 示範
perform	執行 履行
project	專案
initiate	創始 開創
plan	計畫
target	目標 指標
representative	代表
unify	使統一
enlarge	擴大
execute	實行，執行 實施
vivify	使活躍
work	工作
useful	有用的
use	使用 運用
utilize	利用
valuable	有價值的
overcome	克服
top	最高的 最好的

replace	接替	(161)
	替換	
receive	得到	
	接受，收到	
perfect	使改善	
	完美	
motivate	促進	
	激發	
effect	效果	
	作用	
well-trained	訓練有素的	
working model	勞動模範	
excellent league member		
	優秀團員	
excellent party member		
	優秀黨員	

教育背景

education history	教育背景
educational background	
academic history	學歷
level	程度
level of study completed	
	最高學歷
graduate level education	
	研究所學歷
undergraduate level education	
	大學學歷

high school	中學畢業
vocational school	職業學校
secondary education	中學
university	大學
college	大學
others	其它學歷
name of school	畢業學校名稱
address of school	畢業學校地址
name of institution	校名
major	主修
year graduated	年度
period of enrollment	修業年限
name of examination	考試名稱
date (from-to)	學習期間 (從…至…為止)
required years of study	要求學習年限
diploma or degree	文憑或學位
secondary education status	次高學歷狀況
graduated or will graduate from high school / college	已畢業或即將畢業於高中 / 大學
home schooled	在家自學
degree received	已取得的學位
degree earned	已取得的學位

專長、能力

adept in	善於	
mastered	精通的	
good at	擅長於	

推薦、介紹

recommended	被推薦的 被介紹的
be proposed as	被提名為 被推薦為
referee	介紹人
nominated	被提名的 被任命的
be promoted to	被升職為

工作經歷

experience	經歷，經驗
professional	職業經歷
work experience	工作經歷
work history	
occupational history	
previous employment	
employment history	
employment experience	
business experience	
business background	
business history	
professional experience	
employment record	受雇紀錄

specific experience	具體經歷
present employment	現職狀況
position	職位
type of work	工作性質
employer	雇主
period	期間
period of employment	服務期間
responsibilities	工作説明
govt. / state-owned enterprise	公營企業
locally-owned enterprise	私人企業
joint venture	合資企業
foreign-owned enterprise	國際公司
NGO; non government organization	非政府機構

英語能力評鑑

English qualification	英語水平
English language proficiency	英語程度
verbal English	英語口説能力
written English	英語書寫能力
intellectual ability	知能
ability to work with others	協作能力

imagination and creativity	(163)
	創造性
unusually outstanding	
	非常好
fluent	很流利
excellent	精通
distinction	表現優異
superior	優越
good	好
fair	還可以
average	一般
weak	很弱
poor	不好
no information	清楚

英語考試

TOEFL; Test of English as a Foreign Language)	
	托福考試
IELTS; International English Language Testing System	
	雅思測驗
GEPT; General English Proficiency Test	
	全民英檢
TOEIC; Test of English for International Communication	
	多益測驗

工作職掌

employment	工作
position job title	職位
responsibility duty	職責
administer	管理
appointed	被任命的
assist	輔助
export	出口
import	進口

交易屬性

dealer	經銷商
wholesale	批發
wholesaler	批發商
retailer tradesman	零售商
retail trade	零售業
middleman	中間商，經紀人
manufacturer	製造商，製造廠
importer	進口商
exporter	出口商

行業類別

light industry	輕工業	(164)
power industry	電力工業	
automotive industry	汽車工業	
clothing industry	服裝業	
building industry	建築工業	
chemical industry	化學工業	
food industry	食品工業	
oil industry	石油工業	
insurance business	保險業	
communication	通訊業	
electronic industry	電子業	
metal industry	鋼鐵工業	
mining industry	礦業	

● 不同職缺常用單字

發明

design	設計
develop	開發
	發揮
devise	設計
	發明
originate	創始
	發明
inspired	受啟發的
	受鼓舞的

invent	發明
	研究調查
survey research study	調查，研究
test	試驗
	檢驗
verify	證實
	證明
evaluation	估價
	評價
integrate	使結合
	使一體化
introduce	採用
	引進
pattern	專利

維修

maintain	保持
	維修
repair	修復
	修補
standard	標準
	規格
rehash	重新處理

業務

negotiate	談判 (165)
exploit	功勳，功績
create	創造
level	水準
worth	使⋯⋯有價值
realize	了解，實現
goal target	目標
market	市場 行銷
promote	促銷
show	表明，顯示
recover	恢復，彌補
consolidate	合併，匯總
reconsolidate	重新鞏固 重新整頓
shorten	減低，縮短
lengthen	延長

績效數字

double	加倍，翻一倍
redouble	倍增
increase	增加
reduce decrease lessen	減少，降低

spread	擴大
profit	利潤
cost	成本，費用
earn	賺取，獲得
analyze	分析
total	總數，總額
reach	達到
raise	提高

製造

make	製造
manufacture	製造
material	材料，原料
operate	操作(機器等)

採購供需

supply	供給
demand	需求
monitor	監督

輔助協辦

type	打字
sponsor	主辦
strengthen	加強，鞏固
translate	翻譯
recorded	記載的

問題解決

solve	解決	(166)
resolve		
settle		
complaint	抱怨	
claim		
sort out	清理	

管理

direct	指導
eliminate	消除
manage	管理，經營
renovate	革新，修理
innovate	改革，革新
reform	改革
reconstruct	重建
rectify	整頓，改正
lead	領導
guide	指導，操縱
streamline	使有效率 使合理化
systematize	使系統化
regularize	
modernize	
simplify	簡化 精簡
supervise	監督 管理

recognize	認清 辨識
influence	影響
control	控制
significant	意義重大的 影響重大的
conduct	經營 處理
improve	改進 提高
regulate	控制 管理
expedite	加快 促進
speed up	加速
set record	創紀錄
localize	使地方化
authorized	委任的 核准的
break through	驚人的進展 關鍵問題的解決

企業組織結構

organize	組織
establish	(公司)設立，建立
expand	擴張
invest	投資
found	創立

registered	已註冊的	
launch	開辦，開始	
justified	經證明的，合法化	
enterprise	企業	
corporation	股份有限公司	

其他

reinforce	加強，增援
regenerate	刷新，重建
install	安裝
refine	精練，精製，提煉
renew	重建，換新
generate	產生
enrich	使豐富
provide	提供，供應

356

● 校園稱謂

師長

chancellor	大學校長
president	
dean	學院的院長
assistant professor	助理教授
associate professor	副教授
head of the faculty	系主任
faculty	全體教授

teaching assistant	助理
professor	教授
lecturer	講師
counselor	輔導老師
principal	中學校長
headmaster	小學校長
headmistress	小學女校長
teacher	老師

其他人員

secretary	秘書
staff	職員
janitor	工友
contract employee	約聘人員
volunteer	志工

學生

student	學生
guest student	旁聽生
alma mater	母校
alumnus	男校友
	校友
	複數為 **alumni**
alumna	女校友
	複數為 **alumnae**
postgraduate	研究生

		(168)
freshman	大一新生	
sophomore	指大二學生	
junior	指大三學生	
senior	指大四學生	
transfer	轉學生	
special student	特殊學生	
transfer student	轉學生	
audit	旁聽 沒有學分或考試費 用與正式生相同	
exchange student	交換學生	
full-time student	全職學生	
part-time student	兼職學生	
work-study	做校內工作 半公半讀的學生	
international student		
	國際學生	

● 學校制度

考試及作業

homework	作業
assignment	
reading homework	閱讀功課
essay	短文
thesis	論文
paper	
dissertation	

exam	考試
pop test	隨堂測驗
pop quiz	小考
open book exam	開書考試
midterm	期中考
final final exam	期末考
oral test	口試
transcript report card	成績單
flunk, fail	不及格
study plan statement of purpose	讀書計畫

畢業學位

graduation ceremony commencement	畢業典禮
diploma graduation certificate	文憑
degree	學位
Bachelor	學士
Master	碩士
Doctor of Philosophy	博士
Associate Degree	副學士學位
A.A. Associate of Arts	文副學士
A.S. Associate of Science	理副學士

Bachelor Degree	學士學位 (169)
First Professional Degree	初級專業學位
BA; Bachelor of Arts	文學士
BS; Bachelor of Science	理學士
MD; Doctor of Medicine	醫學士
JD; Juries Doctor	法學士
Master Degree	碩士學位
MA; Master of Arts	文學碩士
MS; Master of Science	科學碩士
MBA; Master of Business Administration	企管碩士
M.F.A.; Master of Fine Arts	藝術碩士
LL.M.; Master of Law	法學碩士
MED; Master of Education	教育碩士
Doctoral Degree	博士學位
Ph.D.; Doctor of Philosophy	哲學博士
J.S.D.; Doctor of Judicial Science	法學博士
D.Ed./Ed.D.; Doctor of Education	教育博士
D.Sc./Sc.D.; Doctor of Science	科學博士

教育機構

academic year	學年
early childhood education	兒童教育，多指五歲以下兒童的學齡前教育
day care center **nursery school**	托兒所
family day care	家庭托兒所
preschool	學前班
kindergarten	幼稚園
elementary education	初等教育六年，屬於 **12** 年義務教育
elementary school **primary school**	國小
secondary education	中等教育六年，屬於 **12** 年義務教育
intermediate program **unior high school**	中級教育三年
secondary program **high school**	二等教育三年
senior high school	高中
higher education	高等教育
adult education	成人教育
community college	兩年制大學
junior college	社區大學

two-year college	兩年制學院	(170)
undergraduate	四年制大學	
University	大學	
College	學院 大學的統稱	
Professional school	專業學校	
Graduate school	研究所	

留學考試

TOEFL	托福考試
IELTS	雅思測驗
GEPT	全民英檢
Placement Test	入學前的英文程度 驗
ACT	美國大學入學測驗
SAT	美國學生入學測驗
GMAT	美國商學研究所申 請入學測驗
GRE	美國各大學研究所 或研究機構的申請 入學測驗
MCAT	美國醫學院入學測 驗
LSAT	美國法學院的申請 入學測驗

學校類別

coeducation	男女生同校制度
boarding school	寄宿學校

| private school | 私立學校 |
| public school | 公立學校 |

● 科系課程

數理學科

math mathematics	數學
algebra	代數
geometry	幾何
science	科學 理科
biology	生物
chemistry	化學
biochemistry	生物化學
physics	物理
medicine	醫學
physical geography	地球科學
astronomy	天文學
metallurgy	冶金學
atomic energy	原子能學
chemical, engineering	化學工程
engineering	工程學
mechanical engineering	機械工程學
electronic engineering	電子工程學

文學科

Chinese	中文	🎧171
English	英語	
Japanese	日語	
history	歷史	
geography	地理	
literature	文學	
linguistics	語言學	
library	圖書館學	
diplomacy	外交	
foreign language	外文	
mass-communication	大眾傳播學	
journalism	新聞學	

商學科

commercial science	商學
economics	經濟學
politics	政治學
banking	銀行學
accounting	會計學
finance	財政學
accounting and statistics	會計統計
business administration	工商管理

單字急救包

雅致風靡　典藏文化

親愛的顧客您好，感謝您購買這本書。即日起，填寫讀者回函卡寄回至本公司，我們每月將抽出一百名回函讀者，寄出精美禮物並享有生日當月購書優惠！想知道更多更即時的消息，歡迎加入"永續圖書粉絲團"您也可以選擇傳真、掃描或用本公司準備的免郵回函寄回，謝謝。

傳真電話：（02）8647-3660　　　電子信箱：yungjiuh@ms45.hinet.net

姓名：		性別：　□男　□女	
出生日期：　年　月　日	電話：		
學歷：		職業：	
E-mail：			
地址：□□□			
從何處購買此書：		購買金額：　　　元	

購買本書動機：□封面 □書名 □排版 □內容 □作者 □偶然衝動

你對本書的意見：
內容：□滿意□尚可□待改進　編輯：□滿意□尚可□待改進
封面：□滿意□尚可□待改進　定價：□滿意□尚可□待改進

其他建議：

總經銷：永續圖書有限公司

永續圖書線上購物網
www.foreverbooks.com.tw

您可以使用以下方式將回函寄回。

您的回覆，是我們進步的最大動力，謝謝。

① 使用本公司準備的免郵回函寄回。

② 傳真電話：（02）8647-3660

③ 掃描圖檔寄到電子信箱：

　yungjiuh@ms45.hinet.net

沿此線對折後寄回，謝謝。

廣 告 回 信

基隆郵局登記證

基隆廣字第056號

221-03

 雅典文化事業有限公司　收
新北市汐止區大同路三段194號9樓之1

雅致風靡　典藏文化